D0936119

BLOOD TIES

Center Point
Large Print

Also by James J. Griffin and available from
Center Point Large Print:

Death Stalks the Rangers
Death Rides the Rails
Ranger's Revenge
Texas Jeopardy

**This Large Print Book carries the
Seal of Approval of N.A.V.H.**

BLOOD TIES

A
Texas Ranger Will Kirkpatrick
Novel

James J. Griffin

CENTER POINT LARGE PRINT
THORNDIKE, MAINE

The text of this Large Print edition is unabridged.
In other aspects, this book may vary
from the original edition.
Printed in the United States of America
on permanent paper.
Set in 16-point Times New Roman type.

ISBN: 978-1-68324-962-7

Library of Congress Cataloging-in-Publication Data

Names: Griffin, James J., 1949- author.
Title: Blood ties : a Texas Ranger William Kirkpatrick novel /
    James J. Griffin.
Description: Center Point Large Print edition. | Thorndike, Maine :
    Center Point Large Print, 2018.
Identifiers: LCCN 2018028991 | ISBN 9781683249627
    (hardcover : alk. paper)
Subjects: LCSH: Large type books.
Classification: LCC PS3607.R5477 B58 2018 | DDC 813/.6—dc23
LC record available at https://lccn.loc.gov/2018028991

For Andy and Dina Thomas

BLOOD TIES

1

"I think we're finally nearin' the end of our chase, Pete. Good thing, too. The sun'll be down in less than an hour, so we wouldn't be able to trail those *hombres* much farther tonight," Texas Ranger Will Kirkpatrick said to his horse. "Those are the tracks of the damned stagecoach robbers we've been trailin' over half of the Trans-Pecos, goin' into that canyon up there. They ain't more'n an hour or two old. One of their horses is still wearin' that chipped shoe on his off hind foot, so I know it's the same bunch. There ain't any hoof prints comin' back out, so they haven't doubled back on us.

"Sure wish I knew whether or not that canyon's a box. I'd truly hate to meet all three of 'em unexpected like, when they came ridin' back out. Let's keep movin', fella. But we'd best keep our eyes open. One of 'em might be hangin' back to set up a nice bushwhackin' for us. I don't know about you, horse, but I sure ain't hankerin' to catch a rifle slug in my gut."

Pete snorted, and shook his head. He snorted again.

"I reckon that's your way of sayin' you don't hanker to take a bullet either, Pete," Will said, with a laugh, as he reached forward to pat his horse's neck. "And you're right, you know. A horse is a much bigger target than a man, so a lotta times an *hombre'll* shoot the horse out from under its rider, rather than aimin' for the man. Easier to hit the horse, and once the rider's unhorsed, he's a lot easier target . . . especially if he got hurt or knocked out when his horse went down. I'd sure hate to see that happen to you, pard. We've been together too many years now, goin' back to when we first left home and I signed on with the Rangers. I couldn't ask for a better friend than you, and it'd take me a long time to train another bronc to know his job as good as you do. Well, we'd better get movin'. We sure ain't gonna catch up to those *muy malo hombres* just settin' here. Let's go, boy."

Will lifted the reins along his black and white overo's neck and clucked to the chunky, short-coupled paint, putting Pete into a slow jogtrot. When they had gone about a quarter mile into the canyon, he slowed his horse to a walk.

"We're gonna take it nice and slow from here on in, pal," he told the paint. "Those horse droppin's you just had a sniff at are real fresh. They ain't hardly dried at all, and the flies were just startin' to swarm over 'em. We're gettin' awful close to those outlaws. If I had more sense, I'd leave you here and go ahead on foot, but I sure hate walkin'. Try'n step slow and easy, now. Watch where you plant your feet."

Like most men born and raised to the saddle, Will hated to walk, and avoided it if at all possible. He'd rather take the time to saddle and bridle his horse for a two-block trip in town, even if it took much longer to ready and use his mount rather than his own two feet.

He clucked softly to Pete, nudging him into a slow, deliberate walk. Being practically on top of the men he was after, as near as he could determine, Will no longer had to keep his gaze locked on their horses' hoof prints.

At this point, their trail was clear enough for a half-blind man to follow, anyway. Instead, he slid his Winchester from its saddle boot and held it across the pommel of his saddle. Underneath his sweat stained and battered wide-brimmed Stetson, his brown eyes moved alertly from side to side, scanning his surroundings for any possible sign of a hidden gunman.

Will had ridden about a quarter-mile into the canyon, the hairs on the back of his neck rising and his spine prickling with each bend in the trail, anticipating the pain of hot lead ripping into his back from a drygulcher, unseen behind the rocks, when Pete suddenly stopped. The paint arched his neck and pricked his ears sharply forward. His nostrils flared as he sniffed the air for a scent or sound which Will hadn't picked up yet. Will leaned forward and patted his horse on the side of his neck.

"Shh. Quiet, pal," he whispered. "Now I'm real glad I didn't come in here on foot. Somethin', or more likely someone, is up ahead . . . someone I can't see or hear, but you're tellin' me they're out there and to be careful, just as plain as if you could talk. Good thing I speak fluent horse." After years of having Pete for his mount, Will knew exactly what each action of his horse meant.

Pete blew softly and turned his head slightly. He issued a low nicker so quietly even Will could barely hear it.

"I smell it now, too, Pete," Will whispered. "Wood smoke, and unless I miss my guess, coffee boilin'. I reckon our friends must've decided to call it a night, and set up camp. Wonder if they'll give us an invite to join 'em? Let's just go and find out. Real slow, now."

He touched his spurs lightly to Pete's sides, putting him into a slow walk. A few hundred yards later, Will could see the slightest haze of smoke, coming from just beyond a low rock shelf.

"We caught a break, Pete," Will said. "Seems like those boys must've thought they'd given us the slip. They're about to find out how wrong they were. Those *hombres* sure picked a lousy spot to settle down for the night. We've got the advantage of the high ground. All we've gotta do is ride out on that shelf and we'll have 'em pinned down."

He eased Pete up to the edge of the shelf,

then lifted his rifle to his shoulder. Below him, three men were seated around a small campfire, working on their supper.

"Texas Ranger!" Will shouted. "Don't make a move. I'll put a bullet in the first man who tries."

Two of the men sat there, frozen in place, dumbfounded at seeing the Ranger on the rocks above them. The third jumped to his feet, spilling his tin plate of bacon and beans as he grabbed for the gun on his right hip. Will shot him through the middle of his chest. The impact of the heavy slug slammed the man backward, to haul up against a boulder. He slid to a seated position, his head drooping to his chest, as blood spread crimson over his shirt. A streak of blood from the exit wound in his back stained the rock. Will swung his rifle back to cover the two remaining outlaws.

"Either of you want to get the same?" Will asked them. "If you don't, then just stay hitched."

Both men shook their heads, and kept their hands well away from their guns.

"Good. You're both a sight smarter than your pardner was," Pete said. "Now, stand up. Real slow and easy like."

Both men started to rise. The one nearest the fire edged his hand toward his six-gun. Will put a bullet into the dirt between his feet.

"Try that again, and the next one's plumb in the middle of your chest, just like your pardner got," he warned. "Get on your feet, and don't make a twitch."

"That's better," he said, once the men were standing. "Now, unbuckle your gunbelts, one handed, and let 'em drop. Then kick 'em over by your dead pardner. After that, get your hands in the air."

This time, the outlaws made certain their movements wouldn't be misconstrued. They followed Will's instructions, using just their left hands to unbuckle their gunbelts, and let them fall to the ground. They raised their hands over their heads.

"Now, kick 'em away," Will repeated. Again, the men complied.

"You're both bein' real sensible," Will said. "Now y'all just stand real still, nice and quiet, while I come down there."

He eased Pete over the sloping right side of the rock shelf, keeping his rifle aimed at his captives while he did. He rode up to the men and dismounted.

"Is . . . is Wiley dead, mister?" the younger of the two stammered, swallowing hard before choking the words out. He was merely a youth, a tow-headed, blue-eyed kid who looked to be no more than sixteen or seventeen, and who was now scared half to death. Tears streaked paths through the dirt which coated his cheeks, and his entire body trembled with fear.

"If he ain't, he's the first man I've ever come across who lived with a hole blown clean through his lungs," Will answered. "Yeah, kid, your pard's done for. He didn't have to die, but when he tried for his gun, he left me no choice."

"You didn't have to kill him, Ranger," the other man snarled. He had long, black hair, and brown eyes so dark they appeared almost black. Right now, those eyes glittered with his hatred of the lawman.

"You'd rather I'd let him kill me instead?"

"Now that you mention it, yeah. I wish Wiley'd sunk a slug or two right in your lousy guts."

"Well, mister, I hate to disappoint you, but I wasn't gonna let that happen."

Will pulled his Colt Peacemaker from the holster on his left hip to cover the men, and placed his rifle on the ground.

"Now I'm gonna cuff you both," he said, then nodded at the older man. "You first. Turn around, lower your hands, and get 'em behind your back. One false move, and I'll blow a chunk of your backbone clean out through your belly button. I'm dog tired after chasin' you boys all over half of Texas, I'm not takin' chances with either one of you."

Cursing Will bitterly, the outlaw complied. Once he had turned and his hands were behind his back, Will pulled a pair of handcuffs from his denims' pocket and clamped them around the

15

man's wrists. He removed a heavy-bladed Bowie knife from its sheath on the man's belt and stuck it behind his own pants' waistband.

While Will was securing his partner, the young outlaw, either having screwed up his courage or driven by his fear, made a dive for his gun. He landed on his stomach, grabbed his pistol from its holster and started to roll onto his back, thumbing back the hammer. Will had anticipated the kid might try such a desperate move. Before he could aim the gun and pull the trigger, Will kicked him in the gut. The kid grunted in pain as the air was driven from his lungs. He dropped his gun, wrapped his arms around his middle, and curled up into a ball, whimpering.

"Go . . . go ahead and . . . kill me, Ranger," he gasped.

"I ain't plannin' on killin' you or anyone else, unless you force me to, kid," Will answered. "If you think I wanted to plug your pard, you're wrong. If he hadn't gone for his gun, he'd still be alive. As for you, roll onto your belly, and get your hands behind your back."

Still keeping one eye on the other outlaw, Will waited until the boy was able to roll onto his stomach, and get his hands behind his back. He cuffed the young outlaw, as with the other man removed his knife, then pulled him to his feet.

"Now both of you, get over to your saddles, and sit down," Will ordered. "I'm gonna tie you to 'em for the night. It's too late to start for Pecos now. We'll camp here, then head for town at first light."

"You can't do that, Ranger," the older outlaw protested. "We ain't had a chance to finish eatin' yet. And what if we need to take a leak, or . . ."

"I'll give both of you a chance, one at a time, once I'm certain neither one of you can go anywhere," Will answered. "Now move."

Will had the two men sit alongside their saddles. One at a time, he removed their handcuffs, took the cuffs and locked one end of the cuffs around the saddlehorn fork, the other to each man's right wrist. Once they were secured, he took their lariats, looped one end through the saddle fork and tied it off, then tied the other end around the trunk of a large mesquite. As soon as that was done, he pulled their free hands behind their backs and tied those to their cuffed ones. Finally, he took two lengths of rope, wrapped those around the men's ankles, and bound them tightly.

"There. That should hold you two for the night," he said. "One more thing. Where's the money and passengers' possessions you took when you robbed the stage?"

"You think I'm gonna tell you, Ranger?" the older man said, with a sneer. "Not a chance."

"It's split up amongst all our saddlebags. We didn't take the time to hide it," the younger man

17

volunteered, before Will even had the chance to ask him.

"*Gracias*, kid. I'm obliged," Will said. "Now I'm gonna take care of my horse. Ol' Pete's pretty tired from chasin' you *hombres* over three hundred miles."

"What are you gonna do with Wiley, just leave him for the damn buzzards?" the older outlaw asked.

"I should, and I imagine your pard's beyond carin' about what I do with him," Pete answered. "I'm figurin' he's more worried about what Satan has planned for him right about now. But no, I ain't gonna leave him. Soon as my cayuse is settled, I'll wrap your pardner in a blanket. Tomorrow, I'll haul his carcass into Pecos, along with you two."

Will whistled, and Pete trotted up to him.

"Good boy," he said, as he slipped the bridle off Pete's head. He then removed the saddle and blanket, took a currycomb from his saddlebags, and began grooming the paint.

"I might as well question you two while I'm workin' on Pete," he said to the outlaws. "First, I need your names, bein' as I don't recognize any of you, and I don't feel like goin' through my fugitive list to try'n find if you're in there, seein' as you're both sittin' right there in front of me. It'll be a lot easier if you cooperate, and just answer my questions."

"My name's Kyle . . . Kyle Peterson," the older outlaw said. "That's my brother Wylie lyin' over there, with your bullet in him. I'll get you for gunnin' him down if it's the last thing I do, Ranger. I swear it."

"Your brother went for his gun, after I ordered all of you not to. As far as killin' me, you might want to think hard about that," Will answered. "I don't recollect your name, and from what I understand, no one was hurt when you *hombres* robbed that stage. That means you're only looking at an armed robbery charge, unless I find some other warrants out on you. If you try'n kill me, which I promise you won't be easy, you'll be lookin' at a long stretch in Huntsville for attempted murder of a peace officer. Or hangin' for murder, if you did somehow manage to put a bullet in me."

"Don't matter to me whether I die or not, so long as I send you to Hell first," Peterson replied.

"How about you, son? What's your name?" Will asked the young outlaw.

"It's Jonas Peterson," the boy answered, his voice shaking. "I'm Kyle and Wylie's cousin." His chin trembled as he attempted to keep from crying. "I didn't want any part of this. They talked me into it. I kept tellin' 'em we'd never get away with it. But they wouldn't listen, and kept workin' on me until I finally gave in. I'm a dang fool. What's gonna happen to me, Ranger?"

"That'll depend on a judge and jury," Will answered. "My job is just to make the arrest and haul you in. The court will decide whether or not you're innocent or guilty, and what your punishment will be. My guess is, and you can't hold me to this, if as you say this is the first time you've broken the law, and you ask the judge for leniency . . ."

"Leniency? What's that?"

"It means ask him to go easy on you," Will explained. "I'd hazard you'll only get a short prison sentence, and a stretch of probation time. That means once you get out of jail, you'll have to report in to the local law regularly."

"Don't listen to him, kid," Kyle snapped. "You tried to gun down this Ranger a few minutes ago. I've got to give you credit for tryin'. It took a lot of guts, and it's only too bad you weren't able to get your gun and pull the trigger fast enough. Now you'll be lookin' at attempted murder of a Ranger, in addition to robbery charges. If either one of us gets the chance to kill this son of a bitch, we've gotta take it."

"Ranger?" the boy said, his chin trembling.

"You'll be makin' an even bigger mistake if you listen to your cousin, there," Will said. "I ain't forgotten you tried to plug me, but I'm not gonna bring it up to the judge, unless you force me to. I figure you were just plumb scared senseless. Hell, I probably would've done the same thing, if I were in your boots. I made some real stupid mistakes when I was your age, too. It was pure dumb luck I ended up wearin' a badge, instead of runnin' from one. In fact, quite a few Rangers started out on the wrong side of the law. If you keep your nose clean while you're behind bars, and prove yourself once you're released, you might even think of joinin' up with the outfit some day. You seem to have the guts for the job. It took a lotta nerve to try'n plug me, when I already had my gun in my hand. If you straighten yourself out, you just might make a decent lawman one day."

"He's tryin' to run a sandy on you, Jonas," Kyle said. "Don't believe a word he's tellin' you. Soon as he's got you behind bars, he'll do everythin' he can to make certain you stay there for the rest of your life, if he can."

"I . . . I dunno," Jonas stammered.

"You don't have to listen to me, son," Will said, attempting to keep a note of empathy in his voice, to try and calm the scared young outlaw. "You can take your cousin's word, and try to kill me before I get you to the sheriff in Pecos. I'm only gonna remind you of one thing. Haven't you gotten yourself in enough trouble already, listenin' to your kinfolk? You're just damn lucky it ain't you lyin' dead over there, rather than your cousin. If you keep followin' the owlhoot trail once you're out of prison, I guarantee you sooner

21

or later you'll end up just like Wylie. Dead, with a bullet in you, either from a lawman, or just as likely from one of your pardners when he turns on you. I suggest you think long and hard about that while we're on the way to Pecos."

"I reckon I don't have to," Jonas answered. "I ain't gonna give you any more trouble, Ranger. Kyle, he's right. I never should have listened to you and Wylie. I should have stuck to cowboyin'."

"You just made a real big mistake, kid," Wylie snarled. "Now I'm gonna have to kill *you* along with the Ranger. All it'll take is one bullet apiece in the back."

"Don't let him scare you, Jonas," Will said. "You made the right decision. You won't be sorry, and I appreciate it. When your trial comes up, I'll put in a good word with the judge for you. And you just made my job that much easier. As long as you keep your word, that means I'll only have to watch my back with one of you."

"I ain't afraid of Kyle. Not anymore," Jonas said. "I just want to get this whole thing over with. You certain we can't start for Pecos tonight, Ranger?"

"Nope. We'd be takin' too much of a chance, tryin' to find our way in the dark. There's no moon tonight, so the trail'll be dark as pitch. We'll start out first thing after sunup."

"You ain't gonna live to see another sunrise,

Ranger," Kyle said. "Neither are you, Jonas. I swear it."

"If you try anythin', you'll be a dead man," Will said. "I'm a real light sleeper, and I'll have my gun in my hand. I'd advise you to just get some shut-eye, Kyle. It's an all-day ride back to Pecos."

Kyle's answer was a string of curses.

Will finished caring for his horse. The outlaws had confined theirs in a small side arroyo that had a spring for water and decent grass, always hard to find in this arid part of Texas, so he turned Pete in with them. The paint wandered over to a fair sized cottonwood to scratch his neck on its trunk, then fell to cropping at the grass. After settling Pete, Will wrapped the dead Wylie in a blanket and moved the body behind the boulder where he had fallen.

With that unpleasant chore out of the way, Will rekindled the outlaws' campfire, and cooked his own supper of bacon and beans. He uncuffed Kyle and Jonas, one at a time, to allow them to eat, then go behind some rocks to relieve themselves. Once they were again secured, Will cleaned the dishes and frying pan, and rolled out his blankets. He stretched out on his belly, with his Winchester on one side and his Colt in his right hand. Within ten minutes, he was asleep.

2

Sunrise found Will already awake. Pete nickered to him as he threw back his blankets.

"Good mornin' to you too, pal," Will called to his horse. "Yeah, we're headin' for town, at last. You'll be able to sleep in a real stall and get your belly full of oats and hay tonight. Soon's I take care of business and make breakfast, we'll be on our way. I want to reach Pecos before sundown."

Both of his prisoners were still sound asleep. Will ducked behind some bushes, where he had a bit of privacy but could still keep an eye on the captives, to relieve himself. Once he was finished, he returned to where Kyle and Jonas were still snoring, and kicked each man on the sole of his left boot.

"Time to rise and shine, boys," he said. "We're gonna make Pecos before dark, so we've got to get movin'."

"You might *think* you're takin' us to Pecos, but the only place you're headed is straight to Hell," Kyle answered.

"You're probably right," Will cheerfully agreed, "but I hope not too soon. I ain't in any particular hurry to get there. I'm gonna fix us a quick breakfast, then, Kyle, once I have your brother's body loaded on his horse, I'll get you two mounted up, and we'll be on our way."

Wanting to be certain of reaching Pecos with his prisoners before dark fell, Will didn't make much of a breakfast, but merely boiled some coffee, to go with jerky and some warmed up leftover biscuits. Jonas ate in silence, but Kyle complained bitterly about the meager meal.

"I wouldn't worry about what you're eatin' this mornin' too much," Will finally told him. "Compared to the chow you'll be eatin' behind bars for the next ten or fifteen years, this jerky and hardtack will taste like the best steak from Delmonico's you can buy. So either eat or go hungry. We're pullin' out of here in the next thirty minutes."

As soon as the meal was finished, Will took the blanket wrapped remains of Wylie from where the dead outlaw had been left, and struggled to bend the rigor mortis stiffened body and drape it belly down over the dead man's horse. The animal was none too happy about carrying a corpse, but Will managed to calm it enough to get the body lashed in place. Once that was done, he tied the strawberry gelding to a mesquite, then got the gear on Pete and the other two horses.

"Let's go, Kyle," he said. "I'll get you on your horse first." He untied Kyle's ankles so he could stand up, then climb into the saddle. "And no stallin'."

"All right, all right, Ranger," Kyle muttered. "I reckon you're holdin' all the high cards . . . for now. But I still might have an ace or two up my sleeve." He shuffled slowly toward his sorrel gelding, with Will close behind, his gun aimed at the middle of Kyle's back.

"Get up on your horse," Will ordered, once they reached the animal. Kyle grabbed his horse's reins and pulled on them sharply, causing the sorrel to stumble into him, knocking him backward. Instinctively, Will reached out to break Kyle's fall. When he did, Kyle spun and kneed him in the groin. Will grunted from the impact, dropped his six-gun, grabbed his crotch, fell to his knees, then crumpled onto his side. He curled up into a ball, paralyzed with pain. Kyle picked up Will's gun from where it had fallen and pointed it directly at the center of the helpless Ranger's chest.

"I told you I still had some cards up my sleeve, Ranger," he said, with a sneer. "Now, it's my turn to put a slug in *you*." He thumbed back the hammer of Will's Colt.

"No, Kyle!" Jonas shouted. "Don't do it." Despite still being bound hand and foot, he managed to lunge from where he was sitting, throwing himself at Kyle, rolling, and catching him in the back of the knees. Will's gun fired as Kyle went down, but the shot went wide, the bullet he'd intended for Will instead hitting a boulder, then ricocheting wildly away. Despite the fall, Kyle managed to maintain his grip on the gun. He scrambled to his feet, then grabbed Jonas's shirtfront and pulled him upright.

"I reckon I've gotta take care of you first, kid," he snarled. "Then I'll finish the Ranger." He jerked Jonas against him, both men struggling. The gun in Kyle's hand fired again. The cousins stood there motionless for a moment, then Kyle slumped to the ground, blood staining his shirt where the bullet had entered his belly, and darkening the right leg of his pants where it had lodged in his thigh after its journey through his intestines and pelvis, puncturing the femoral artery. His eyes were wide in shock and disbelief.

"You . . . you done . . . killed me, kid," he choked out. He struggled to rise, but fell back, too weak to do anything but moan. His eyes glazed over as he lost consciousness, his body twitching while he bled to death.

Wordlessly, Jonas took Will's gun from Kyle's hand, and turned toward the still helpless Ranger.

"Go ahead and finish me off, boy," Will said, his voice still tight with pain. "No one'll ever figure out what happened to me and your cousins. By the time what's left of our carcasses, after the scavengers are finished with 'em, are discovered, if they ever are, you can be safe in Mexico, or up in the Indian Territories. So go ahead. Plug me and get it over with."

"I ain't gonna kill you, Ranger," Jonas answered. He put Will's gun down on a flat rock. "I meant what I said yesterday. I'm through bein' an outlaw. Lemme help you get up."

"All right," Will said.

As best he could, since he was still handcuffed, Jonas slid his arms under Will's shoulders, helping him to a seated position.

"Lemme rest just a minute," Will asked, when renewed pain shot through his groin and into his belly.

"Sure, Ranger," Jonas agreed. "You gonna be okay?"

"Yeah," Will said, with a grunt. "It ain't gonna be too comfortable sittin' a saddle for the next few days, though."

"Ouch." Jonas grimaced.

"That's a damn understatement, if ever I've heard one," Will said. He managed a rueful grin. "Gimme a hand gettin' all the way to my feet. I think I'm ready."

"Sure."

Jonas again lifted Will by the shoulders. Once he gained his feet, Will stood, swaying. As soon as he felt steadier, he picked up his gun from where Jonas had placed it.

"*Muchas gracias*, Jonas," he said. "I owe you one. Your cousin had me dead to rights, and there wasn't a thing I could do about it. I'll be sure the judge knows you saved my life. I can't believe I was that dumb, lettin' Kyle get the drop on me that easy."

Pete snorted and bobbed his head up and down, as if agreeing with his rider.

"When I want your opinion, I'll ask for it, horse," Will said. "Reckon I am lucky at that. Makin' such a damn stupid mistake could have cost me my badge . . . or gotten me a bullet in the belly, if it hadn't been for Jonas, here. I reckon we're both obliged to him, since I doubt you'd've been happy seein' me gunned down. After all, nobody else is gonna put up with your shenanigans, and your constant beggin' for doughnuts."

"Since I kept you from bein' shot, can't you just let me go, Ranger?" Jonas asked.

"I wish I could, but I'm afraid not, son," Will answered. "First of all, I'm a lawman. That means I'm sworn to uphold the law, no matter what. Second, even if I wanted to, there were witnesses on that stage; the driver, shotgun, and passengers, who all saw three holdup men. It'd look a mite suspicious if I only brought in two dead men, and tried to claim the third had gotten away, especially since I didn't take a slug. Plus, those folks gave me pretty good descriptions of the three of you, eye and hair color and so forth, even though you were masked. They described your horses and outfits pretty good, too.

"Even if I did let you go, it's likely someone else would recognize you, and bring you in. Even worse, Wells Fargo would put out a bounty on you. That'd put the bounty hunters on your trail. I don't need to tell you most of those just as soon bring you in dead as alive. A lot of 'em, probably more so dead. It's a lot easier to haul in a dead man, rather'n have to keep an eye on a prisoner until you get to the nearest town with a jail.

"You might not believe me, but you're better off takin' your chances with me, rather'n bein' turned loose, or tryin' to make a break for it. At least I'll be able to try'n talk the judge into goin' easy on you. If you do try to run for it, and somehow manage to get away from me, you'll be lookin' behind your shoulder for the rest of your life, wonderin' whether a lawman or bounty hunter is on your trail. Let me bring you in, and I'll do everythin' I can for you. Does that make sense?"

"Yeah, I guess it does at that, Ranger. Damn," Jonas answered, clearly not convinced. "Besides, I reckon I missed my chance, anyway. You've got your gun back, and I'm still handcuffed. If I was dumb enough to try'n escape, you'd just plug me in the back and be done with it."

"No, I wouldn't. There's no way I'd ever shoot a prisoner of mine in the back. As far as lettin' me take you in, you'll find out I'm right, in time," Will said. "We're wastin' daylight. I'll get Kyle's body loaded on his horse, then, soon as you're mounted, we'll be on our way."

Will began to drag Kyle's body toward his horse. As he did, the tension which had built up in Jonas as he and Kyle struggled left him, to be replaced by a sick feeling, deep in his gut. He began to tremble, and all the strength seemed to drain from him. His knees buckled, and he doubled over, using his hands and locking his elbows to brace himself from dropping face-down to the dirt. He vomited up what little he had eaten for breakfast, continuing to dry heave even after the contents of his stomach were emptied.

"You gonna be all right, Jonas?" Will asked, once the youngster's stomach had finally settled enough so he could speak.

"Yeah . . . yeah, I guess so," Jonas answered. "It's just that . . . Hell, I've never had to kill a man before, let alone gun down my own cousin. I dunno . . . how I'll get over that."

"You'll never get used to killin' a man—at least, I haven't, and most of the other lawmen I know never have, either," Will answered. "I still get a sick feelin' in my gut every time I have to take a man's life. But, some men don't give you a choice, then there are others that just need killin'. And don't forget, if you hadn't shot Kyle, you'd be lyin' here dead right now, rather'n him. So would I, which means Kyle would probably have killed more people before someone finally stopped him.

"Lemme get you some water. I'll finish loadin' up Kyle while you get your nerves unjangled. Soon as you're ready, I'll get you on your horse. I'm still aimin' to make Pecos before dusk. I'm not gonna bother to cover Kyle. That'll save a bit of time."

"All right," Jonas answered.

Will retrieved his canteen, and let Jonas have a good, long swallow. He left the canteen with the young outlaw while he tied Kyle's body on his blaze-faced sorrel. After that, he helped Jonas onto his blaze-faced bay gelding.

"Sorry I have to keep you cuffed and tied to your saddle after you saved my life, Jonas. But I really don't have any choice. And even now, I still can't be one hundred per cent certain you won't try'n make a break."

"I understand, Ranger," Jonas answered. "All I want right now is to get outta here and get this over with."

"Then, we'll head out," Will said. He had tied Wylie's horse to Kyle's, and fastened a lead rope to Kyle's. He picked up the end of the rope, and swung into his saddle. "Let's go."

3

While they rode along, Will questioned Jonas about the stagecoach robbery.

"Why'd you and your cousins decide to start robbin' Wells Fargo stages, Jonas?"

"It wasn't my idea. It was Wylie and Kyle's, mostly Kyle's," Jonas explained. "You see, I'm the only kid my folks ever had. My ma and pa had a small spread outside of San Angelo. Wylie and Kyle's folks, my Aunt Gertrude and Uncle George, had another one, about five miles from ours. When I was only eleven, the fever took my ma and pa, and then the bank took the ranch. I had no choice but to move in with my aunt and uncle.

"My uncle has always been pretty much no-account. My aunt tried her best, but Wylie and Kyle took after their pa, and she never could teach 'em much. She finally up and left a couple of years ago. Went back East somewhere to live with her sister. Once she was gone, the place really went to Hell. My uncle quit doin' the little work he had been, and just spent most of his time drinkin'. One day, he was all of a sudden gone. I reckon he just up and drifted.

"Wylie and Kyle worked the place for a while, but finally decided hard work wasn't for them, neither. They managed to bring in enough money from gamblin' to keep us in beans and bacon, but eventually, even that ran out. That's when they decided to rob a bank or stagecoach. They settled on the coach, thinkin' it would be easier, with a lot less folks around, rather than hittin' a bank in the middle of town. I guess they didn't count on a Ranger bein' close by." Jonas paused, and shook his head. He turned to look back at the bodies. "I never should've let them talk me into throwin' in with 'em. I mean, I knew what we was doin' was wrong, but I finally gave in. Should've just saddled my horse and ridden away. Reckon it's too late, now."

"You're right about one thing," Will said. "You can't undo that robbery, but you *can* turn your life around, if you want. Don't be too hard on yourself. You're just a kid, and you made a dumb mistake. And you're still alive, which is more than I can say for your cousins. Let's see what happens after I talk with the judge."

Jonas merely shrugged, then rode in silence with his head bowed the rest of the journey to Pecos.

Most times when Will rode into a town, the majority of people on the streets didn't give him so much as a second glance. There was nothing about his appearance that would mark him as a Texas Ranger. Instead, he resembled just another drifting cowboy, probably one riding the chuckline, going from ranch to ranch looking for work, but never sticking at one spread for very long.

While Texas Rangers didn't wear uniforms, and few wore badges, Will was one of the growing number who *did* carry a badge, the silver star in silver circle design favored by the famed lawmen. He'd commissioned a Mexican silversmith in Del Rio to carve his from a Mexican five peso coin. However, he usually left it hidden in his shirt pocket until needed. A Ranger made plenty of enemies, and that silver badge made a nice, shiny target. There was no sense inviting an outlaw's bushwhack bullet right through your shirt's left chest pocket by advertising you were a Ranger.

Will was a couple of inches taller than average, and lean. He had light brown hair, and slightly darker eyes of the same hue. He was only twenty-eight, but years of exposure to the harsh Texas sun and wind had added some age to his appearance. An old bullet scar along his right cheekbone stood out starkly white against his sun-bronzed skin.

Right now, his jaw was stubbled with two weeks' worth of whiskers, and his hair hung over his collar. He wore his gray Stetson, sweat and dirt stained, a blue-and-white-striped shirt, with a roughout leather vest over that, and denim pants. Around his neck was looped a red checked bandana. His boots were black, scuffed and well worn. On his left hip hung a .45 Colt Peacemaker—on his right, a sheathed Bowie knife. An 1873 Winchester was in the saddle boot under his left leg.

Pete, his overo paint, was a bit unusual for a range rider, since most cowboys favored solid colored mounts, disdaining spotted horses as fit only for Indians or women, but still not that outstanding that he would attract much attention. Pete's nondescript appearance belied the fact that he had plenty of speed and endurance. The gelding could go for days on little water and snatches of grass.

So, when Will reached Pecos about four in the afternoon, no one would have even taken notice . . . if it weren't for the two horses trailing him, carrying two dead men, and the young man riding alongside him, handcuffed, with his ankles tied to his stirrups. As he headed down the main street toward the Reeves County Sheriff's Office, a crowd began to assemble and follow, some of its bolder members shouting out questions. Will ignored them, until he reined up in front of the office. Amos Pettengill, the county sheriff, had heard the commotion, and was standing in front of his door, holding a shotgun and watching Will approach.

"I dunno who you are, cowboy," Pettengill said, as Will reined up, "but you'd better have a damn good explanation for what I'm seein' here. I don't appreciate strangers ridin' into my territory with two dead men lashed to horses trailin' him."

Pettengill was a big, burly man in his early forties, slightly shorter than Will, but more muscular. Only the slightest hint of a paunch pushed out his gunbelt. A huge, flowing dragoon moustache adorned his upper lip. His piercing, almost dark-as-black brown eyes glared at Will from under a flat-brimmed, high crowned hat. Clearly, he could handle any trouble which came his way. Amos Pettengill was not a man to be trifled with.

Will returned the sheriff's glare with one of his own. He reached into his shirt pocket, pulled out his badge, and pinned it to his vest.

"Texas Ranger Will Kirkpatrick, Sheriff. As for your 'damn good' explanation, these are the *hombres* who held up the San Angelo stage forty miles outside town. I'd been trailin' 'em for almost ten days. They led me on a chase through the badlands for fair. When I finally cornered 'em, one of 'em made the mistake of goin' for his gun. I had to plug him.

"This mornin', when we were startin' for town, I made a mistake when I took my eyes off his pardner for a minute, and he managed to get the drop on me. If it hadn't been for this young feller ridin' alongside me, I'd be coyote grub right about now.

"However, out here in the street is no place to talk about any of this. I'm tired and sore, and my horse is tired, which means we're both plumb wore out. I just want to get my prisoner in a cell, get these two bodies to the undertaker, and get Pete a stall and good feedin'. Then I want a shave, haircut, and bath for myself, followed by a good meal and a soft bed in a decent hotel room. I also need to get the stolen money to the bank for safekeepin'. It's in the horses' saddlebags. Is that good enough of an explanation for you?"

"I reckon it is," Pettengill answered. "I also reckon I owe you an apology, Ranger. Amos Pettengill's my name. I had a bad night last night, tryin' to chase down a couple of horse thieves, who still managed to disappear into the malpais. I reckon I took out my mad on you, and I'm sorry."

"No apology needed, Sheriff," Will answered. "I guess I came off a mite rough, too. Seems like we're both tired. If you'll just take this prisoner off my hands, then tell me where the undertaker's at, and let the banker know I need to use his vault, I'd be obliged."

"There's no need for you to haul those carcasses to the undertaking parlor," Pettengill answered. He pointed at two men, and signaled to a third, who wore a town deputy marshal's badge. "Curly, Fred. Take those bodies down to Monahan's. Tell Mort he's got a couple of customers, and that the county'll be payin' for the buryin'. Leave their horses and gear with Casey at the livery. Tell him the usual arrangement. The county will sell the animals and gear for his board and the funerals."

He pointed to the man wearing the town deputy's star. "Harry, since the marshal's outta town, take the money off the Ranger's hands and tell John Slater to put it in his vault. Unless you have any objections, Ranger."

"None at all." Will shook his head.

"Fine. Then get down offa your horse, and bring your man inside. I'll pour you a cup of coffee while we start the paperwork."

"Sounds good to me."

Will dismounted, looped Pete's reins over the rail, and gave the horse a pat on the neck.

"You're gonna have to stay here a mite longer, Pete," he told the paint. "Soon as my business with the sheriff is finished, I'll get you a stall and a good feed. Extra oats and hay for you tonight, pard."

Pete shook his head and snorted. Will chuckled.

"Time to get you in a cell, Jonas," Will said. He walked over to Jonas's horse, removed Jonas's bonds, and helped the young outlaw dismount.

"Right this way," Pettengill said, swinging open the door to his office. Will and Jonas followed him inside. Pettengill removed a ring of keys hanging from a peg, and used one to unlock a heavy oak door, which led to a row of cells. He opened the first one vacant.

"In there, you," he told Jonas. Jonas walked into the cell and laid on his back on the bunk.

"Can you get my prisoner some water, Sheriff?" Will asked. "It's been a long, hot ride for both of us."

"Sure, soon as we get him logged in," Pettengill answered. "He'll be gettin' his supper in about an hour, from the Pecos Café across the street. It won't be anythin' fancy, but it won't be slop, like so many other jailers serve their prisoners."

"That's good to hear," Will said. "As soon as we get the paperwork out of the way, I'd like to talk to you about this boy."

Pettengill turned and gave Will an odd look.

"Why? Somethin' I should know about him?"

"We'll talk in your office, Sheriff. Jonas, I know it won't be easy, but try not to worry, at least, not too much. With any luck, I can get this whole thing straightened out."

"All right, Ranger," Jonas answered, hopelessness evident in his voice.

"Let's go, Sheriff," Will said.

He and Pettengill returned to the office. One of Pettengill's deputies had just returned.

"Mike, this is Ranger Will Kirkpatrick," Pettengill said. "Ranger, Mike Hardy, my chief deputy."

The two men nodded at each other.

"The Ranger here just brought in a prisoner," Pettengill continued. "He's in cell four. Would you mind fetchin' him some water?"

"Not at all, Amos," Hardy answered. "Good to meet you, Ranger."

"Same here," Will replied.

"Grab yourself a cup of coffee and pull up a chair, Ranger," Pettengill offered. He handed Will a tin mug. "You mind if I call you Will?"

"Not at all."

"Good, then call me Amos. No point in bein' formal," Pettengill said. He poured himself a cup of coffee from the pot on the stove, then sat behind his spur-scarred desk, opened a drawer and removed three forms, then placed them on the desktop. Will also poured a cup of the black, steaming brew, reversed a straight back chair, placed it in front of Pettengill's desk, then straddled it.

"Two of these are for the dead men," the sheriff said. "We'll get to those after we take care of the paperwork on your prisoner." He picked up a pen and dipped it in the inkwell on the corner of his desk.

"Now, what's the young renegade's name?"

"Jonas Peterson."

Pettengill scrawled the name on the form.

"Whereabouts is he from?"

"He claims his folks had a ranch down below San Angelo. When they passed, his aunt and

43

uncle took him in. They also had a ranch in the same area. Their kids were his cousins."

"You said *were* his cousins, Will?"

"Yeah. They're the two jaspers on their way to the undertaker."

"Understood. What are the charges?"

"Armed robbery."

"That's all? No murder, attempted murder, or resistin' arrest?"

"Nope. No one was hurt when they held up the stage, not even the shotgun guard. Seems like he didn't put up much of a fight, which was probably the smart thing to do, but sure won't endear him to his bosses at Wells Fargo. From what I understand, only two shots were fired. And the boy didn't try to resist when I finally caught up with him and his kin. Good thing he didn't. You saw what happened to the other two."

"Might've been easier all around if he had, and you'd plugged him, too," Pettengill said. He slid the form across the desk and handed Will the pen, then opened his center desk drawer and took out another. "You know the routine. Fill out the complaint section and sign it. While you do that I'll make start fillin' in the other forms for the coroner. What were the other two jaspers' names?"

"Kyle Peterson, and Wylie Peterson."

"And you caught up with 'em in Reeves County?"

"Sure enough did."

"*Bueno*. That'll simplify things, at least a bit. No jurisdictional problems. I'll fill in what I can, then you'll have to do the rest."

"I'm obliged, Amos. Sooner we can get this business done, the sooner I can settle my horse and myself."

Forty minutes later, the papers were completed and filed. Will tilted back in his chair and sighed. Pettengill refilled his pipe, and touched a match to it.

"You said you wanted to talk to me about your prisoner, Ranger," he said, once the tobacco was burning. He took a puff on the pipe, then blew a smoke ring toward the ceiling. "Would you like to get some supper first? We could head across the street to the café. Mebbe you could tell me what's on your mind over a good steak."

"I'd rather not talk in public," Will answered. "You said the café provides your prisoners' meals, if I recollect."

"That's right, they do."

"Tell you what. If it's okay with you, would you mind having them send over our supper, along with Jonas's? That way, we can eat, and also discuss his situation in private."

"I don't see why not," Pettengill answered. He called to his deputy, who was stationed at the front desk.

"Mike."

"Yessir, Sheriff," Hardy answered.

"Me'n the Ranger, here, are gonna have our supper in the office tonight. You mind goin' for our meals?"

"Not at all," Hardy answered. The tone of his voice indicated he'd really rather not go get the suppers, but he knew from years as Pettengill's deputy, he had no choice. "What're you gonna have?"

"Steaks and spuds for both of us, along with whatever kind of beans Miss Sally has tonight. How do you want your steak cooked, Will?"

"Nice and seared on the outside, still red on the inside, if it can be managed," Will answered.

"Not sure how it'll turn out," Hardy said. "Miss Sally's chuck is all right, but she's not the best cook. Most folks eat there simply because May Pardee, who runs the only other restaurant in town, is even worse, plus she's ugly as sin, to boot. At least Sally Johnson's easy on the eyes. And her coffee is real good. May's is more like dishwater."

"I'm not the best cook, either," Will answered. "After weeks on the trail eatin' my own cookin', I'm sure however Miss Sally cooks my steak, it'll taste just fine."

"Same thing for the prisoner, Sheriff?" Hardy asked. Will answered him instead.

46

"Yes, Deputy. If there's any apple pie, order me and Jonas a slice of that, also."

"Is that all right, Sheriff?" Hardy questioned his boss.

"As long as the Ranger says so, yeah," Pettengill answered. "You might as well order your supper too, Mike. Get the same for yourself, also."

"All right. You want pie, too?"

"Silly question, Mike."

"Yeah, I know," Hardy said, grinning. "Four orders of steak, taters, beans, and apple pie. Along with a pot of coffee. I'll be back in half an hour or so."

"That's fine, Mike."

"Take your time, deputy. There's no hurry. While you're pickin' up our supper, I'm gonna take my horse to the livery stable and get him settled in. Ol' Pete's pretty tired, and deserves a good rubdown and feedin' after chasin' Jonas and his kinfolk practically to Hell and back. I'll just get him a stall and his supper, and give him a quick brushin' until later. I'll be back by the time you return."

"You know your way to the livery?" Pettengill asked.

"Yup," Will answered. "I've passed through Pecos a couple of other times. Never had cause to stop in your office since I was on my way elsewhere. Joe Bates knows how I want my horse taken care of. Pete'll be in good hands. I'll see you shortly."

Will and Hardy left together, the deputy heading across the street to the café, while Will untied Pete, climbed into the saddle, and rode his tired gelding toward the stable.

"You'll rest good tonight, Pete," he told the horse, with a pat on the shoulder. "Mebbe a couple of nights, dependin' on what Austin has lined up for us next. C'mon, let's get you tucked in."

He put Pete into a slow trot.

Will usually groomed Pete himself whenever he put the horse up at a livery stable. However, he'd put Pete up at the Bates Livery several times previously, and knew the owner, Joe Bates, would take good care of his mount. He did stop by Marie's Bakery, just as the owner was locking up, to buy Pete two leftover doughnuts. Once Will's horse had his treat, he ran a currycomb over him to remove the heaviest dirt and dried sweat, then left him in Joe's capable hands. He was back at the sheriff's office slightly more than forty-five minutes after he'd left. Pettengill and Hardy were already working at their meals.

"We were wonderin' where you got yourself off to, Will," Pettengill said. "Your supper's keepin' warm on the stove."

"I stopped by the bakery to get my horse some doughnuts before I took him to the stable. Pete

48

always looks for doughnuts when we're in a town," Will explained. "Plus, I always take a few minutes to say goodnight to him."

"Sure sounds like you spoil that horse, Ranger," Hardy said. "It's just a bronc, after all. Horses are made for work, that's it. Soon as you wear one out, you send it off to the renderin' factory, then get yourself a new one. Simple as that."

Will's face visibly darkened in anger. He struggled to keep his temper in check, his voice even.

"You're wrong, Deputy, and if you treat your horses like that, some day you just might be dead wrong. Yeah, I probably do spoil Pete, I'll admit it. However, he's saved my life more'n once, and he's the one friend I can count on, no matter how tough things get. When you depend on your horse as much as I do, and when you spend weeks on the trail, sometimes with only him to talk to, you find out right quick that a good horse ain't just another animal. He's a friend, companion, and pardner. One thing I can't abide is anyone mistreatin' a horse."

Pettengill broke in, before the mounting tension between the Ranger and his deputy could escalate into something more serious.

"Will, you said you wanted to talk with me about the prisoner you brought in. Is that for me and you alone, or can Mike stay and finish his supper?"

Will thumbed back his Stetson and ran a hand through his hair before answering.

"I don't guess it'll do any harm to let him stay. What I'm gonna bring up will all be public soon enough."

"All right, then. Go ahead," Pettengill said.

"Sure." Will cut off a piece of his steak and popped it in his mouth before continuing. "That is, if I don't bust my jaw on this hunk of leather. Must've come from a real old cow."

"I warned you Miss Sally wasn't the best cook, but she's runnin' the only halfway decent restaurant in town," Pettengill answered, chuckling. "Doesn't give us much choice, unless you want to sample some of my cookin', which is even worse, I promise you that. Since my wife passed, I would have plumb starved to death if it weren't for Sally. See if you can spit out your story without any broken teeth."

Will grimaced when he bit down on a particularly tough bite of his steak. He spit the gristly, inedible, half-chewed piece onto his plate.

"I'm not gonna go over the whole story, Amos," he said. "Jonas Peterson doesn't seem like he's really a bad kid. He's been more scared than anythin' else, from the moment I tracked him and the other two down. He just was forced into bad company when his ma and pa died, so he had to go live with his no-account kinfolk, from what he told me. He didn't want to take part in

50

that stagecoach robbery. His cousins talked him into it."

"Could be he's just runnin' a sandy on you," Pettengill said. "With both his cousins dead, there's no one to back up his story . . . or contradict it."

"That could be, but I don't think so," Will said. "When his cousin Kyle got the jump on me, the kid saved my life by stoppin' him before he could plug me. In the fight for my gun, Jonas ended up killin' his own kin. I was still helpless, lyin' on the ground doubled up in pain, when Jonas got my gun back. He could have shot me on the spot, and gotten clean away. Instead, he gave me my gun, told me he was done bein' an outlaw. Said he was gonna let me take him in and face the consequences. Besides, like I said, the entire time he was scared half to death. The boy just doesn't have the makin's of a renegade. However, if he ends up in Huntsville, he will, and fast. You'n me both know that's no place for a kid."

"The Ranger's right, Sheriff," Hardy agreed. "I hate it when I have to escort a man to Huntsville. The place gives me the willies, and I've been a lawman long enough there ain't much that bothers me. But that place makes my skin crawl, every time."

"So what're you sayin', Will?" Pettengill asked. "You just want to let the kid go?"

"Not at all," Will answered. "What I'd like

51

to do is stay here in Pecos until Jonas's trial is held. However, as soon as the Western Union office opens tomorrow morning, I'll have to send a telegram to Austin, letting Headquarters know this case is solved, and asking where they want me to head next. I'm certain they won't allow me to hang around here very long, not with so many outlaws still on the loose, all over Texas.

"So, Amos, this is where you come in. I'm going to write a deposition for the court tonight, explaining all the circumstances surrounding the robbery, the part Jonas took in it, and how he helped me when he could just as easily have put a couple of slugs in my belly, and hightailed it for Mexico or the Indian Territories. I'll be askin' the judge to grant Jonas clemency, or at least leniency, since he was influenced by his older cousins, who really didn't leave him much choice; he admitted his mistake and wants to make up for it, and that he saved my life when he could just as easily have let his cousin kill me, or killed me himself.

"I'm goin' to leave that with you to present to the judge when Jonas comes to trial. I'd like to ask you to make certain the judge receives the deposition, and explain to him for me how strongly I believe that Huntsville isn't the place for the boy. I'd hope the judge would give him probation, or at the most a short prison sentence that he can serve right here in Reeves County."

Pettengill sucked on the ends of his moustache before answering, then gave Will a slight smile.

"I'd be happy to do that for you, but it won't be necessary. The circuit judge arrived in town earlier this afternoon. He'll be holdin' court in session for the next three or four days, dependin' on how fast he clears the cases waitin' for him. You can talk to him yourself, first thing in the mornin', before court starts. I'll introduce you to him."

"What kind of judge is he?" Will asked.

"Ambrose Huttwelker? He's tough, but fair. His family came over here from Germany when he was just a kid, from what I understand. He's gruff, like a lotta Germans, but not a bad *hombre* at all. He'll listen to you, I can promise you that. Which is more than I can say for a lot of judges, I might add."

"Well, if I can speak to him myself, things might go better for Jonas. I'm obliged, Amos."

"No problem. I'd hate to see a kid who has a chance to turn his life around sent to Huntsville. He'd come out a hardened criminal."

"If he came out at all," Hardy added. "A place like Huntsville is real hard on a kid. Like as not he'd get killed by another prisoner, or end up hangin' himself in his cell. Jonas seems like a decent sort. He was real polite when I brought him his supper. He'd never make it in Huntsville."

The three men finished the rest of their meal in silence. Will drained the last of his coffee, then pushed back from the table.

"Where you headed now, Will?" Pettengill asked.

"I'm gonna check and see if the barber shop's still open," Will answered. "If it is, I'm gonna get myself a long overdue shave, haircut, and bath. Then I'll get a room at the hotel across the street for the night."

"That sounds good to me, Ranger," Hardy said. "Wish I could, but I'm on duty all night. The Pecos marshal's short a man, so he asked me to cover the town tonight. Mebbe I'll see you tomorrow."

"Mebbe," Will answered. "You be careful."

"Always am, plus I've been a lawman in these parts for years. I know most of the troublemakers, and can usually spot any newcomers who might try'n stir things up."

"I'm gonna call it a night soon as my other deputy shows up," Pettengill said. "Will, be here at eight, if that's not too early. We can have breakfast, then I'll take you to meet Judge Huttwelker."

"I dunno if I'll be able to eat breakfast," Will answered. "This steak is sittin' in my gut like a hunk of granite. Sure hope it doesn't block things up."

"I have to admit, Sally's cookin'll do that to

a man who ain't used to it," Pettengill said. He shook his head. "Either that, or it'll go through him like corn through a goose. I hope you're not too sick to meet the judge come mornin'."

"I'll be there, sick or not," Will answered. "I've just gotta stop by the telegraph office and get my wire off to Austin first, then I'll see you right here. *Buenos noches.*"

"G'night. See you in the mornin'," Pettengill said.

"I'll walk with you as far as the barber shop," Hardy offered. "Mose should still be open. If he's closin' up, I'll talk him into takin' one last customer."

"I'd appreciate that," Will said.

"Good. Sheriff, I'll see you tomorrow evenin'," Hardy said.

"G'night, Mike. See you then."

The barber was working on his final customer for the day when Will walked in. "Have a seat," he invited, "I was just gonna close up after Mister Adams here, but I've always got time for one more patron."

"I'm obliged," Will said. He took off his hat, hung it from a peg, then settled in the nearest chair. "Does that include time for a bath, too?"

"Even if it didn't, the way you look and smell, I'd *make* time," the barber answered, grinning to take the sting out of his words. "Pardon my sayin' so, but you sure need one. My name's Moses . . . Moses Hanson. But everyone in town just calls me Mose. And this here's Quincy Adams. He's the president of our bank."

"No offense taken, Mose," Will answered, with a smile of his own and a nod to the two men. "I reckon I am lookin' a mite rough. Been on the trail for several weeks, now. Texas Ranger Will Kirkpatrick."

"Texas Ranger, huh?" Adams said. "You have business in Pecos?"

"Yeah, but I'll only be in town for a day or two," Will answered. "I caught up with a trio of stage robbers some miles out of town. I brought them in . . . well, *one* of 'em, anyway. He's in a cell at the county jail right now. The other two are already at the undertaker's, I'd hazard."

"Probably good riddance," Adams said.

"The two dead ones, yeah," Will agreed. "I'm not so sure about the third one. He's just a kid, and it seems his kin forced him to help them. We'll have to see what the judge says."

"You're all finished, Mr. Adams," Mose said, as he pulled off the cloth covering the banker. "I'll see you in a week."

"As always," Adams said. He paid the barber, nodded to Will, then stepped out into the gathering darkness.

"I'm ready for you, Ranger," Mose said. Will settled in the barber chair, then pulled out his gun and set it in his lap before Mose put the cloth over him.

"I guess you can't be too careful when you're a lawman," Mose said.

"That's right," Will answered. He settled back while Mose adjusted the hair, stropped his razor, then built up a fresh mug of lather.

"Just relax," he told Will, when he took the first stroke. He began a running line of talk.

It turned out Mose was a freed slave, who had drifted west from Louisiana after the war. He told Will he'd been taught to read by one of the house servants, and learned the barbering trade from another slave on the same cotton plantation. He, like most barbers, was an interesting conversationalist and pleasant company.

By the time Will had been barbered, shaved, and bathed, he felt like a new man. He left Mose fully relaxed. Once he had checked on Pete for the night, then collapsed onto his bed at the hotel, he fell instantly asleep. Between the long days on the trail and the cleanup at Mose's shop, he would sleep the night through.

4

The next morning, Will checked on Pete, then went to the Western Union office. He had to wait almost thirty minutes for the telegrapher to arrive. Once he did, Will composed a message for Headquarters, and watched the telegrapher send it, waiting for confirmation that the telegram had indeed gone off. Once that was done, he returned to the sheriff's office. Amos Pettengill was waiting for him, along with another man.

Pettengill glanced at the Regulator clock ticking away on the wall behind his desk.

"There you are, Will. I was hoping you'd be on time, and you're not too far off," he said. "You don't still have a bellyache from Miss Sally's cookin', do you? Because I just sent Mike over to her place for ham, eggs, and fried spuds. Grab yourself a cup of coffee, in the meantime."

Will headed for the stove, took a tin mug from the shelf next to it, and poured himself a cup of the thick, black brew.

"Nah, my belly survived, but I do figure takin' a bullet in the gut probably'd hurt less than eatin' another of her steaks," Will answered. "As far as bein' late, I apologize. I had to get my wire off to Austin, and I had to wait for the clerk at the Western Union office to open. I was there early, but he showed up late, fifteen minutes after he was supposed to be there. Soon as I made certain he sent the wire, I hustled right over."

"Don't worry about it," Pettengill said, with a wave of his hand. "We still have plenty of time before court opens. I'd like you to meet Judge Ambrose Huttwelker. Judge, Ranger Will Kirkpatrick."

"I'm pleased to meet you, Judge Huttwelker," Will said, as he and the judge shook hands.

"I might say the same, Ranger," Huttwelker answered. He was a big, burly man, with thick burnsides that ended in muttonchop whiskers. His hair and beard were salt and pepper gray. Behind the spectacles perched on the bridge of his nose, he had piercing blue eyes. "Sheriff Pettengill, here, tells me you'd like to speak to me about the prisoner you brought in yesterday."

"That's correct, Judge."

"The sheriff has already explained to me a little about the situation. If you could just fill me in a bit more while we wait for our meal to arrive."

"I took the liberty to give Judge Huttwelker some of the basics about your prisoner, Will," Pettengill said. "I hope I didn't get out of line."

"I hope not, but I'm sure whatever you told him won't really make a difference," Will answered. "Let's hear what he has to say, then I'll know. Judge . . ."

"Ranger Kirkpatrick, I understand, from what

Sheriff Pettengill told me, you apprehended three stage coach robbers. Two of them resisted arrest, and were subsequently killed by yourself. The third, a young man, surrendered without incident. Am I correct so far?"

"You are, Judge," Will answered.

"Furthermore, I also understand you wish to have the young man granted leniency. Is that true?"

"Yes. You see, not only didn't he resist arrest, he saved my life, when one of his pardners jumped me, and managed to get my gun. Jonas stopped him, and nearly got killed himself. After that, he could have gunned me down, but he didn't. He gave me back my weapon, told me that he was through bein' an outlaw, and was goin' to plead guilty and face his punishment."

"Hold it right there," Huttwelker said. "You've given me enough so I have a general idea of what happened, and why you believe the young man should be granted leniency. It's my opinion the rest of your statement should wait until the preliminary hearing, so it will be entered into the record as official testimony. I'll hold off my thoughts until then. Do you understand?"

"I do. And I'd prefer it that way," Will answered. "I'd rather wait and bring the details out in court."

"Then we're in agreement," Huttwelker said.

"Just in time, too," Pettengill said, as Mike Hardy walked through the door, carrying a red-checked cloth covered tray. "Here's Mike with our breakfast."

While breakfast wasn't quite as awful as supper had been, the eggs were runny, the ham and potatoes greasy. Luckily, Sheriff Pettengill brewed an excellent cup of coffee, one of the best Will had ever tasted. Still, his stomach was queasy as he took his place in the courtroom. Will was grateful Judge Huttwelker had moved Jonas's case to first on the docket, because he had a feeling before too long he'd have to make a very fast dash for the outhouse.

Courts and trials here on the Texas frontier were far more informal proceedings than back East, or even in the larger cities of the West Coast. When Judge Huttwelker entered the small courtroom, the spectators stood. He merely indicated they should sit down with a wave of his hand.

Deputy Hardy was standing by the bench, as the sole bailiff. With opportunities for entertainment in small towns like Pecos—even though it was the Reeves County seat—being limited, when court was in session the room was usually packed to overflowing. Today was no exception.

"Court's in session. You all know my name, Judge Ambrose Huttwelker. You also know I'll tolerate no outbursts or disturbances in my

62

courtroom." He slammed down his gavel on the desk, then picked up a file.

"The first case is the State of Texas versus Jonas Peterson. This is just a preliminary hearing. Is the defendant present?"

"I am, Your Honor." Jonas's voice shook as he answered.

"Please take the witness chair."

"Yes, sir, Your Honor." Jonas, his head bowed, shuffled to the witness stand.

"Bailiff, please swear in the witness."

"Yes, Your Honor."

Mike Hardy held out a Bible. "Place your hand on the book, son."

Jonas complied.

"Do you swear to tell the truth, the whole truth, and nothing but the truth, so help you God?"

"I do."

"Please be seated," Huttwelker ordered. "Do you have an attorney?" he continued, once Jonas was in the witness chair.

"No, Your Honor."

"You are aware, son, that you have the right to an adequate defense. This court will appoint an attorney to represent you, if you cannot afford one, or find one who will take your case."

"I am, Your Honor. But I don't need one. I'm guilty, and admit I helped take part in the robbery I'm accused of."

"I see," Huttwelker said. "Does that mean you

are waiving your right to a trial by a jury of your peers?"

"If that means I don't want to sit through one, yeah," Jonas said. "I mean, *yes,* Your Honor."

"Are you certain?"

"Yes, Your Honor."

"Then this will be a trial, rather than a preliminary hearing. Please state your name for the record."

"Jonas Daley Peterson."

"Mr. Peterson, since you intend to plead guilty as charged, do you wish to make a statement, before I pronounce sentence?"

"Yes, Your Honor. I just want to say that I wish I'd never gotten involved in this robbery. I'd like to apologize for takin' part in it. If the folks who were on that stagecoach were here, I'd apologize to them, too. I know it's not an excuse, but I let my cousins talk me into helpin' 'em rob the stage. I never should've listened to 'em, no matter how much they pleaded with me, or threatened me if I didn't go along. Now they're both dead, and I'm goin' to prison. I'm ready to take what's comin' to me, and once I get out, I'm gonna find me an honest job."

"I see," Huttwelker said. "I have a question for you, Mr. Peterson. You stated your cousins threatened you, if you refused to take part in their scheme? Let me remind you that you are under oath."

"Yes, Your Honor. They told me, since I knew what they were planning, that if I didn't go along, they'd have to kill me, to make certain I didn't go to the law and turn 'em in."

"Well, that's certainly a mitigating circumstance," Huttwelker noted. "Do you have anything else you wish to say?"

"No, Your Honor."

"Very well. You may step down. Remember that you remain under oath until the conclusion of this hearing."

"Yes, Your Honor."

Jonas left the witness chair and returned to his seat.

"The court now calls Texas Ranger William Kirkpatrick to the stand," Huttwelker said. "Please approach the bench, Ranger Kirkpatrick."

Will pushed himself to his feet and walked to the witness stand.

"Bailiff, swear in the witness," Huttwelker ordered.

"Yes, Your Honor." Hardy held out the Bible. "Ranger, place your hand on the book."

Will did so.

"Do you swear to tell the truth, the whole truth, and nothing but the truth, so help you God?"

"I do."

"Please be seated."

"For the record, state your name and occupation," Huttwelker said.

"Texas Ranger William Kirkpatrick, ordinarily attached to Company C, Frontier Battalion, but currently assigned at large to Texas Ranger Headquarters in Austin."

"You were the arresting officer in the case before this court?"

"Yes, Your Honor."

"Briefly, tell the court the circumstances of this arrest."

"Of course. Eleven days ago, I received a report that the San Angelo stage was held up, forty miles south of here. I rode to the site of the holdup, found the tracks of three horses, apparently the outlaws', and took on their trail. I finally caught up to 'em the day before yesterday. I ordered them to surrender. One of 'em, who I found later to be a Wylie Peterson, went for his gun. I had to plug him. The other two men gave up without resistance."

Jonas looked up at Will, startled. For his part, Will hoped no one in the courtroom, particularly Judge Huttwelker, noticed Jonas's look of surprise.

"Please continue, Ranger," Huttwelker said, when Will hesitated.

"Since it was late in the day, with dusk coming quickly, I chose to camp for the night, and start for Pecos in the mornin'. I secured the two surviving men, Jonas Peterson, who is the man on trial here, and Kyle Peterson. As Jonas has already testified, Wylie and Kyle were his cousins. After making supper for myself and my prisoners, I secured them for the night, then got some much needed rest."

"What happened the next morning?"

"I'm comin' to that, Your Honor. After making a quick breakfast, I prepared to transport my prisoners to Pecos for incarceration in the Reeves County jail to await trial. Unfortunately, while I was gettin' Kyle Peterson on his horse, he managed to get the jump on me. He got his hands on my gun, and was goin' to shoot me down, when Jonas interfered. He told Kyle not to kill me. Kyle then threatened to shoot both of us.

"Jonas fought with him, they struggled, and when Jonas attempted to wrest my gun from Kyle's grasp, it went off. The bullet penetrated Kyle's belly, went through his pelvis and exited from his groin, then lodged in his right leg. The slug apparently penetrated a major artery or vein in the leg, because Kyle rapidly bled to death. He died almost instantly. He would have died in any case, bein' gut-shot at point blank range.

"Jonas could have killed me on the spot. Instead, he gave me back my gun, and told me he was through being an outlaw. So he's here, on trial for armed robbery, when he could easily have fled to Mexico or the Indian Territories."

"Let me get this straight, Ranger. I'd like a few more details, if you wouldn't mind providing them. You stated Jonas prevented his cousin Kyle from shooting you. Are you saying this young man, on trial here, saved your life?"

"Yes, he did."

"I would like to hear the specifics of everything that led up to his doing that, if you wouldn't mind, Ranger."

"Not at all. Although, it's kind of embarrassing, since I made a damn greenhorn mistake. When I was gettin' Kyle mounted on his horse, he jerked the animal's reins, causing it to stumble into him. He started to fall, or so I thought, and I made the mistake of instinctively trying to catch him. When I did, he spun and kneed me right in my nu . . . um, my horse chestnuts."

"Quiet," Huttwelker ordered, when the spectators broke into laughter.

"Continue, Ranger. And please refrain from cursing in my courtroom."

"I'm sorry, Your Honor. Needless to say, I was helpless with the pain. I dropped my gun, went down, and curled up in a ball. Kyle picked up my gun and was gonna plug me. There wasn't a thing I could do to stop him. But, even though he was still handcuffed, Jonas jumped him before he could pull the trigger. When he and Kyle fought for the gun, it went off.

"Luckily for both me and Jonas, Kyle took the slug. I figured for certain that Jonas then intended to kill me. In fact, I told him to plug me and get it over with. He shook his head, said he meant it when he told me he was through with bein' an outlaw. He put my gun down, and soon as I was able, he helped me stand up. Once as I was ready to ride, we started for Pecos. He gave me no trouble the entire trip, nor did he give the sheriff or deputies any problems when he was jailed."

"I see," Huttwelker said. "I take it you are saying the young man's actions during and since his arrest should be taken into consideration when I hand down his sentence."

"I am, Your Honor. I'd hate to see a young man like Jonas sent to Huntsville for a long prison term. I'm sure you're aware what would happen to him there. He'd have to fight every day for survival, and most likely as not would come out a hardened criminal, if he lived to be released at all. Very few men who are sentenced to Huntsville turn their lives around, and become honest citizens."

"I am indeed familiar with the conditions at Huntsville State Prison, Ranger Kirkpatrick. And, as you say, Mr. Peterson's actions with you are mitigating circumstances that should indeed be taken into consideration. However, they do not excuse the fact he did participate in an armed robbery. It's quite possible, if the driver, shotgun guard, or any of the passengers on the stage had attempted to resist, there might very well have been murder committed."

"I know that, Your Honor. However, the fact remains, there were no shots fired, Jonas cooperated with me at all times, and in fact, as I've mentioned more than once, he did save my life. He also could have escaped, but made no attempt to do so. I did forget to mention he also told me where to find the stolen money and passengers' possessions, when his cousin Kyle refused to do so. I realize some kind of punishment is in order. So does Jonas. However, I am asking if he has to spend time in jail, he be allowed to serve his sentence right here in the Reeves County lockup."

"I understand your concerns, Ranger, and will certainly take them under advisement," Huttwelker said. "Do you have anything further to say?"

"Only that Sheriff Pettengill and Deputy Hardy'll also vouch for Jonas, if you'd like to add their testimony to the record," Will answered.

"I don't believe that will be necessary," Huttwelker answered. "You're dismissed, Ranger. But you are still under oath."

"Thank you, Your Honor. I'm obliged."

"I've heard all the testimony I need to make a decision in this case," Huttwelker said, once Will had returned to his seat. "Jonas Peterson, if you would stand."

"Yes, Your—Your Honor, sir," Jonas answered, stammering in his fear. He came to his feet.

"Jonas Peterson, first, I am going to ask you one final time, are you pleading guilty to the robbery of the San Angelo-Fort Stockton-Pecos Wells Fargo stage?"

"I am, Your Honor."

"Then I am ready to impose sentence," Huttwelker said. "I have heard the law officer who arrested you, Texas Ranger Will Kirkpatrick, speak very highly on your behalf. I have no doubt, if, as Ranger Kirkpatrick testified, under oath, you had not taken the actions you did, Ranger Kirkpatrick would indeed have been shot dead by your cousin, Kyle Peterson. Your own sworn testimony has also convinced me that you were an unwilling, or at least reluctant, participant in the crime. However, nonetheless, a serious crime was committed, one in which you took part. Justice demands you must be subjected to punishment for that crime. Do you understand me?"

"Yes, Judge—I mean, Your Honor."

Jonas's shoulders sagged, and his eyes welled up with tears.

"The minimum sentence for the crime of armed robbery is five years," Huttwelker said. "Therefore, I am sentencing you to five years in state prison. However, due to the extenuating circumstances, first, your being pressured and threatened by your cousins, second, the assistance you provided to Ranger Kirkpatrick, preventing his murder and assuring Kyle Peterson was not able to escape justice, I am suspending the sentence. That means, as long as you obey the terms of the sentence and keep out of trouble, you will spend no time behind bars."

"Thank you, Your Honor." Jonas's voice broke.

"Let me finish," Huttwelker said. "As a condition of your sentence, you will be placed on probation for one year. For that year, you will be in the custody of Texas Ranger William Kirkpatrick. Do you understand?"

"I . . . I'm not certain, Your Honor."

"That means you must remain with Ranger Kirkpatrick, or be where he can keep in contact with you, and know your whereabouts, at all times."

Will sprang to his feet. "Hold on just a damn minute, Judge, before you saddle me with this!"

"Yes, Ranger Kirkpatrick? You do realize you're out of order? And that you just cursed in my courtroom, for the second time?" Huttwelker said, his displeasure at being interrupted clear in the tone of his voice.

"I guess I am, and I apologize, Your Honor," Will said.

"Apology accepted. Speak your piece, Ranger."

"I can't babysit Jonas for a whole year, much as I'd like to help the kid," Will said. "I'm a da . . . um, *dang* Texas Ranger. I don't know where I'll be from one day to the next, let alone whether or not I'll even live through a day. I can't have Jonas traipsin' along with me everywhere I go. And I sure can't keep an eye on him when I'm tryin' to arrest an outlaw, or worse yet in a gunfight with a band of renegades. It'd be impossible."

"I understand your objections, Ranger; nevertheless, those are my terms. Either you assume custody and responsibility for Mr. Peterson, or he goes to state prison for five years."

"But exactly how am I supposed to do that, *and* my job?" Will objected. "I'd be worried all the time he might catch a slug meant for me."

"I don't know, but you'll have to figure that out, if you want the boy to have a chance. You yourself are the one who said he didn't deserve to be sentenced to prison, that he should be given a chance to turn his life around. My opinion is, to be given that chance, he needs the proper guidance. My feeling is *you* are that proper guidance."

"But, exactly how do you think I'll be able to pull that off?" Will asked.

"Again, I don't know," Huttwelker answered. "Hell, make him a damn Texas Ranger. The outfit is always short of men. And I know plenty of good lawmen who started out on the wrong side of the badge . . . including a number of Rangers."

A few of the spectators burst into soft snickers at hearing Huttwelker curse, just after he had scolded Will for doing the exact same thing.

"Order," Huttwelker said, slamming his gavel for emphasis. "Ranger, what about that idea?"

"Mebbe it'd work if Jonas was old enough, Judge," Will conceded, "but he's still a boy. And I'd have to clear it with my captain. I don't have the authority to sign on a new man, just to temporarily deputize one."

Huttwelker turned his attention back to Jonas.

"Mr. Peterson?" he said.

"Yes, Your Honor?"

The hope which had flared in Jonas's eyes, when he'd thought there was a chance he would not be going to prison, had been replaced by a look of total dejection.

"How old are you, son?"

"I turned eighteen two months ago, Your Honor," Jonas answered. "The date's written in my ma's Bible, which is still in my saddlebags, unless someone took my stuff from the livery stable. That Bible is all I have left to remember my ma and pa by."

"There you have it, Ranger," Huttwelker said to Will. "He might not look it, but the boy's eighteen, old enough to enlist with the Rangers. As far as your not being able to enlist a man, once court is over for the day, I'll prepare and sign a letter for your commanding officer, explaining the reasons for my decision. Will that be satisfactory?"

Will rubbed his jaw before replying. "I reckon

it will, Your Honor. The only thing I'd ask you to add would be that, if anythin' should happen to me, or if for some reason I receive an assignment where it would be impossible for Jonas to stick with me, that Captain Hunter will be allowed to place him in the custody of any available man."

"That's reasonable, and prudent, considering the somewhat short life expectancy of any lawman, particularly a Ranger," Huttwelker agreed. "Jonas Peterson, I accept your guilty plea to the charge of armed robbery, and hereby sentence you to five years in state prison, aforesaid sentence to be suspended. You are also placed on probation for one year, in the custody of Texas Ranger William Fitzpatrick, or any other Ranger his commanding officer chooses. You are also to join the Texas Rangers, pending approval of . . . What is your commanding officer's name, Ranger Kirkpatrick?"

"Captain Paul Hunter."

"Captain Paul Hunter. If Captain Hunter does not agree, or if you violate any terms of your probation, you will be taken into custody immediately, and sent to Huntsville State Prison for the full five years. Do you understand?"

"Yes, Your Honor," Jonas answered. "I'll do as you say. I sure don't want to spend five years behind bars."

"Fine," Huttwelker said. "You understand, young

man, I am giving you a chance to turn your life around, and an opportunity to make something of yourself. I have never before let anyone who has come before my bench on such a serious charge off so lightly. The only reason I have chosen to do so in your case is the testimony of Ranger Kirkpatrick, and the willingness of Sheriff Pettengill and Deputy Hardy to also vouch for you. In addition, I, too, sense you are a decent individual, who was led by bad companions into a terrible mistake. Don't show us that we were all wrong about you."

"I sure won't, Your Honor," Jonas answered. "I promise you that."

"That's all I ask," Huttwelker said. "Remain here in this courtroom until I end the morning session for dinner. I'll prepare the letter at that time. That's all. Next case."

Jonas returned to his seat next to Will, and sat down. He gave an audible sigh of relief.

"Ranger, thanks for stickin' up for me," he whispered to Will. "I won't let you down."

"I hope not," Will said. "You ain't found out yet what you let yourself in for, yet. Once you start chasin' outlaws, and they start shootin' back at you, you just might wish you'd taken the five years in Huntsville."

He grinned, trying to reassure the boy, but Jonas could tell Will was deadly serious. Becoming a Texas Ranger just might be the toughest choice he'd ever made. However, facing five years in Huntsville instead, he knew he didn't have any choice at all.

"What do we do now?" Jonas asked Will, as they walked out of the courthouse. Will had folded the letter signed by Judge Huttwelker and shoved it in his vest pocket.

"We'll stop by the telegraph office and see if there's a reply to my wire to Headquarters," Will answered. "After that, Jonas, I figure on stoppin' at the closest saloon and havin' a couple of beers. Mebbe with any luck, I'll be able to talk the barkeep into fixin' us some ham and eggs or somethin'. I dunno about you, but my stomach can't take another meal from that café."

"Mine can't, either," Jonas agreed. "Not that I was able to eat all that much, what with worryin' about what was gonna happen to me. Now that I know, my belly's grumblin' that it ain't been filled, but I don't want it feelin' like I swallowed a brick, neither. Like it did last night."

"Well, everythin' ain't quite settled yet," Will reminded him, as they started down the street. "I've still gotta convince Cap'n Hunter to take you on."

"Do you think that'll be a problem?" Jonas asked. "After all, it's only my whole life you're talkin' about."

Will shook his head.

"Nah. It won't be. The Rangers are usually short a few *hombres*. It's hard to recruit men who'll work for low pay, bacon and beans, and ammunition, just to get shot at by renegades who'll do whatever they need to keep out of jail. Everythin' else, horse, clothes, guns, whatever, comes out of our pockets. The state will replace your horse if it gets shot, but that's about it. The hard part, for you, begins after you're sworn in. That's when we'll find out whether you've got the stuff to stick as a Ranger."

"Do you think I'll be able to?" Jonas asked.

"I dunno. There's no way to tell until your first real confrontation with a band of desperadoes," Will answered. "You showed a lot of sand when you stood up to Kyle, and when you didn't plug me and run when you had the chance. It took a lot of guts to turn yourself in, too. I'd say you'll do just fine."

He pointed to a chipped adobe building half a block away, sporting a freshly painted sign which read "Cactus Cal's Saloon" in bright green letters. A painting of a prickly pear cactus in full bloom was the most prominent feature of the sign, the plant's brilliant yellow blossoms complementing nicely the tan of the adobe. "Meantime, there's our saloon. And here comes the Western Union operator. Seems like we won't have to stop at the telegraph office after all."

The clerk was hurrying toward Will and Jonas, waving a thin sheet of yellow paper.

"Ranger! I've got the reply to your wire," he shouted. He was puffing for breath by the time he reached the two men. "I'm glad I found you, since I knew it was urgent you received the answer the moment it came in."

He shoved the yellow flimsy into Will's hand.

"I'm obliged," Will said. He dug in his pocket and handed the clerk a nickel. *"Gracias."*

"What's it say?" Jonas asked, as Will scanned the contents of the brief message.

"I've been ordered to return to Austin as fast as possible," Will answered. He crumpled the paper and shoved it in his shirt pocket. "I'll receive my next assignment there. Damn. I hate the thought of havin' to go all the way back to Headquarters, then probably be sent right back out this way again. But, that's probably gonna be for the best. I'd rather have Cap'n Hunter meet you in person, rather'n havin' to try'n convince him by telegram to add you to the roster.

"Well, now that that's settled, we'll have our beers, then wander over to the Texas and Pacific station to get tickets for ourselves and our horses on the next eastbound train. We'll ride the T & P to Fort Worth, then take a local to Austin. It'll take a couple of days, but that's still better'n ten days hard ridin'. Let's get those beers, and hopefully, some chuck. And since we'll be ridin' together, you might as well start callin' me Will."

They headed inside Cactus Cal's. It took a moment for their eyes to adjust to the dimly lit interior after the bright west Texas sun. The saloon wasn't much different than any other west Texas barroom, with a long, mirror-backed bar, gambling tables, a small dance floor, and a beat-up piano. This time of the day, the place wasn't busy. A couple of percentage girls lounged in one corner, sipping at glasses of tea. They wouldn't begin on watered down drinks until the evening crowd began to arrive. Other than the two women, the only other occupants were a black swamper, who was mopping the floor and spreading fresh sawdust, and the bartender, who looked up as Will and Jonas bellied up to the bar.

"Howdy, gents," he greeted. "I'm Cal Collins, the owner of this sorry establishment. What can I get you fellers?"

"Two beers," Will answered. "And if you have 'em, some ham and eggs. I can't take another meal from that café where the sheriff gets his grub."

"You do need an iron stomach to down Sally's cookin'," Collins agreed, with a grin. "Say, I recognize you fellers now. You're the Ranger who was in court this mornin', and the young outlaw you brought in. It was mighty fine of you, Ranger, stickin' up for this young'n, when you could have just let him spend the next few years behind bars." He extended his right hand. "I'd like to shake your hand. You too, kid."

"Sure," Will answered, as he took the proffered hand. "And it wasn't a big deal. After all, the kid *did* save me from takin' a couple of slugs right through my brisket. Seemed like the least I could do to return the favor was try'n keep him outta Huntsville. The names are Will and Jonas."

"Well, I'm pleased to meet you both," Collins said, as he and Jonas shook hands. "The beer ain't cold, but it ain't too warm, either. I can rustle up some ham and eggs for you, too. Even got some bread and butter to go with 'em."

"That'll be just fine," Will answered.

"Comin' right up."

Collins drew two mugs of beer and set them on the bar, then disappeared into the kitchen. A moment later, the delicious aroma of frying ham and eggs came drifting into the barroom. Will took a sip of his beer.

"This ain't bad at all," he said. "Let's sit down."

He and Jonas took seats at the closest table. The two percentage girls wandered over, and eyed the rugged pair.

"Would you boys like some female company?" one asked. "I'm Lila, and my friend's Estrella."

Lila was a full-figured green-eyed blonde, dressed in a sequined blue satin dress. Estrella was Mexican, with flowing black hair and flashing black eyes. She wore a white, low cut peasant blouse, and a flowing, multi-colored striped skirt.

"Sure. We'll buy you dinner and a drink, if you want," Will agreed. "We won't be here long enough for a dance, or anthin' else, though. We've gotta catch the next train to Fort Worth. I'm Will, and this here's Jonas."

"Charmed," Lila said, as she took the chair next to Will. "The piano player doesn't come in until four, anyway. And the meal sounds good. Charley," she called to the swamper.

"Yes, Lila?" he answered.

"Tell Cal to put on two more orders," Lila said.

"Make that three," Will added. "Have him cook one for you."

"Yessir, Ranger," Charley answered. "I surely do appreciate that." He leaned his mop against the bar, then went into the kitchen.

"*Muchacho*," Estrella said to Jonas, "If you have to pass the time, you might as well do so in the company of a beautiful woman, *si*?" She kissed him on the cheek.

"*Si . . . si*," Jonas stammered. He blushed bright red.

Cal's ham and eggs, while not the best food Will had ever tasted, were still far better than the meals from the Pecos Café. With a decent meal behind his belt, and a couple of beers in his belly, Will was in a much better frame of mind when he and Jonas left the saloon than he had been when they arrived. That wasn't to last very long, however.

Rather than walking to the other end of town, the two men had gotten their mounts out of the livery stable, and ridden to the Texas and Pacific depot. They dismounted, looped the horses' reins around the hitchrail, and went inside. There was a lone clerk on duty behind the iron-grated ticket window. He looked up, and pushed back the green eyeshade on his forehead as they approached.

"Good afternoon, gents," he said. "How might I help you?"

"Howdy. Texas Ranger Will Kirkpatrick. We'll need two tickets on the next train to Fort Worth, with a transfer to Austin," Will answered. "We have to reach Ranger Headquarters as quickly as possible. We'll also need a cattle or box car for our horses."

"I'm sorry, but I'm afraid you won't be going east by train," the agent said. "There were some bad storms east of here a couple of weeks back. They caused some flash floods. The bridge over the Pecos was weakened so badly it can't hold the weight of a train, until emergency repairs are completed. In addition, there are several smaller trestles that have been washed away completely. Westbound trains are only going as far as Abilene, for at least another week. Eastbound trains are stopping here. You could ride to Abilene, then pick up a train to Fort Worth there. Or take the stage by way of San Angelo."

"Either way'd take as long as ridin' direct all the way to Austin," Will said.

"Sorry again, Ranger." The ticket agent shrugged. "The Texas and Pacific Railroad has a lot of power in this state, but none with Mother Nature. Wish I could give you better news."

"No need to apologize," Will answered. "It's not your fault. C'mon, Jonas. It looks like we're ridin' to Austin after all. I reckon we'd better stop at the general store to stock up on supplies. Then swing by the telegraph office to send a wire to Cap'n Hunter, and let him know we can't take a train. Good thing I didn't give up my hotel room yet, either. You can bunk with me tonight. We'll be leavin' at first light. Let's go."

5

After bidding farewell to Sheriff Pettengill and Deputy Hardy, Will and Jonas left Pecos shortly after seven o'clock the next morning. Jonas had refused Will's offer to let him stop at Kyle's and Wylie's graves before they left town. He'd said as far as he was concerned, he wished they'd never been his kinfolk.

"It's a three-day ride until we reach the next town of any size. That's Granada. We'll camp for the next couple of nights, Jonas," Will said, "then stop there, before we have to cross the Pecos. Granada's not much of a place, just a few buildin's put up as a supply point for some ranches that were started in the area a couple of years ago. There's no hotel, but the saloon has a room in the back with two or three beds for rent. That'll be the last time we sleep under a roof until we reach Austin. More importantly, there's a livery for our horses. They'll need a good night's rest and feed before we hit the Pecos at Horsehead Crossing."

"Horsehead Crossing? I've heard stories about that damn ford," Jonas said. "It's supposed to be one helluva place to try'n cross the Pecos."

"It is, but it's the only decent crossing within sixty miles or more," Will said. "I've used it a few times, so I've got a good idea how to make it across safely. It's dangerous, but we'll manage. Now, there's no waterholes between here and the Pecos, except a few too alkaline or salty to drink, so we'll have to go real easy on our water, since all we'll have is what's in our canteens, for both us and our horses. That's another reason we have to go by way of Horsehead Crossing. The Comanches found the only waterhole anywhere for miles around at that spot. When we do get there, make certain your horse don't try'n drink from the Pecos, no matter how thirsty he is. The river's water ain't fit to drink. It's too briny, and'll poison a horse . . . or man."

From Pecos to Austin was just over four hundred and fifty miles. Covering that distance on horseback, at the usual mileage of thirty per day, meant the journey would take fifteen days. Pushing a horse to its limit, a man could average approximately fifty miles per day. However, few horses could keep up that grueling pace. Usually, a mount pushed that far would break down before reaching the end of the journey—or, if it did survive the trip, would be wind-broken or crippled, ruined for the rest of its life. For the first two hours of their ride, Will studied Jonas and his horse, trying to determine just how hard he dared push the young man, and, more importantly, his mount.

Jonas still didn't look eighteen years old to

Will. However, the family events recorded in the Bible he carried did indeed confirm his birth date. He also handled his horse well, much as any man who had worked cows from a young age. Rebel, his horse, also seemed sturdy enough. The gelding was a well-muscled bay, who had a narrow blaze down the center of his face, and white stockings on his right front and left hind legs. He'd handled the fairly quick pace Will was setting with no trouble.

"Jonas," Will finally said, "I'd like to make it to Austin in ten days, eleven at the most. That means we'll have to cover a bit more than forty miles a day. Do you think you can handle that hard a pace, for that long?"

"I'll be able to keep up, don't worry about that, Will," Jonas assured him.

"What about your horse?"

"Rebel? Don't worry about him." Jonas reached forward and patted the bay's neck. "You can handle just about anythin' I ask of you, can't ya, boy?"

Rebel twitched his ears and snorted.

"See. He'll do just fine."

"Good. Then let's get movin' a bit faster."

Will kicked Pete into a lope.

The next three days were a hot, dusty ride over the arid high desert terrain of the Trans-Pecos. Except for an occasional mesa or butte in the distance, and scattered dry washes or shallow arroyos, the land was sandy and almost table flat. The vegetation consisted mainly of scrub brush, mesquite, various cactus such as prickly pear and cholla, and tough, drought-tolerant desert grasses. A few junipers, and even an occasional stunted oak, could be found in the rare spots, or on the higher elevations of the mesas, where the soil held enough moisture to allow them to survive.

After spending the night at Granada, where they picked up a few more supplies, plus fleas from the infested mattresses at the Granada Saloon's back room, they left at first light to continue their trip. Nearly two hours later, they reached Horsehead Crossing. Will had set an easy pace this day, knowing the horses would need all their strength to make the hazardous crossing of the Pecos.

"Damn!" Will exclaimed, as they reined in. "The river's runnin' a lot higher'n I figured on."

"I was hopin' you wouldn't say that," Jonas answered. "What're all those horse skulls doin' stuck up in the mesquites?"

"Those are from horses that died tryin' to make the ford, either from drownin' or gettin' stuck in quicksand," Will answered. "Comanches first used this crossin', near as anyone can remember. Someone, sometime in the past put up a horse skull, then more men who lost horses or mules here did the same. That's how this ford got the name Horsehead Crossin'."

"How about now? Do you think it's too dangerous for us to try'n cross?" Jonas asked.

"I dunno." Will studied the roiling, muddy Pecos as it ripped through its bed, foaming and churning. He thumbed back his Stetson and ran a hand through his hair.

"Well?" Jonas said.

"We don't have any other choice," Will answered. "There's not another decent crossin' for sixty miles or more. Since we don't have any idea when the river will go down, or whether it's still risin', for that matter, we're gonna have to chance it. How good do you swim?"

Most cowboys swam poorly, if at all, and many had an innate fear of deep water. On cattle drives, far more men died from drowning when fording a herd across a swollen river than from stampedes, snakebites, gunshots, or other mishaps.

"Fair to middlin'," Jonas answered.

"What about your horse?"

"He's done okay the few times we've herded cows across a creek."

"This sure ain't no creek," Will said. He spat into the dirt.

"I kinda noticed that," Jonas said, with a rueful grin. "Just exactly how do you propose we get across?"

"With a lot of luck, prayers, and the Good

Lord's help," Will said. "I can usually tell where the quicksand's at, but the water's so high I can't spot any. In one way, that's good news, because we won't have to slide our horses too far down the steep banks, then climb the other side, since the river's bank full. The minute we put our broncs into the water, they'll have to start swimmin', so it's unlikely they'll get trapped in any quicksand. The bad news is they'll have to fight the current all the way across, then somehow get enough footin' to scramble out on the other side, before the current carries 'em downstream. And with the river in flood, there's liable to be all sorts of snags, most of which we won't be able to see until they're on top of us. A half-submerged log can knock you right outta your saddle, break your horse's ribs, or push him under the surface, so you'll both drown. Then again, of course, there's always the chance of water moccasins or rattlesnakes that got caught up in the flood. They'll be damn scared, and damn mad, so they'll strike at anythin' that gets in their way. Huntsville startin' to look better to you yet, Jonas?"

"I'll let you know after we make it across . . . *if* we make it across." Jonas shook his head. "Well, I guess there's no point in waitin' any longer."

"No, there ain't," Will agreed. "You say you've never crossed a deep, fast runnin' river before?"

"Nope," Jonas answered. "Just a few creeks,

where Rebel had to swim for a couple of hundred feet at most, but that's all."

"Then I'm gonna have to give you a quick lesson," Will said. "Get off your horse."

"All right."

Jonas and Will swung out of their saddles.

"Pull off your boots, tie 'em together, and hang 'em over your saddlehorn," Will instructed. "That way, if you get swept off of your horse, and do have to swim, you won't have waterlogged boots draggin' you down. Take off your socks and stuff those inside your boots, if you want. I know a lotta men who'd rather strip to the skin when fordin' a river, figurin' if they did end up havin' to swim they wouldn't have any clothes weighin' 'em down. That's not a bad idea if you're followin' a herd, and you can put your clothes and guns in the chuck wagon and float 'em across. But if we took off our duds, bundled 'em up with our guns inside, and tied 'em to our saddles, we'd risk losin' everythin' if we got separated from our horses. So we'd better make certain we don't."

"You make it sound as easy as shootin' fish in a barrel," Jonas said.

"Yeah . . . a barrel tumblin' over a waterfall, and no hook on the line," Will said. "Another thing. If your horse does begin to struggle, get outta your saddle and swim alongside him. Hold on to the horn so you don't get separated. Or drift back and grab onto his tail. Let him pull you along until you reach the other side. If he's in trouble, he's more likely to get out of it without your weight on his back. Understand?"

"That does make sense, at least, sorta," Jonas agreed. "Long as I keep clear of Rebel's hooves."

"That's right, although a kick while he's swimmin' wouldn't be quite so bad, since the water would take a lotta the power out of it. Of course, if you got kicked in the head, that'd probably still knock you senseless, but if you were that far underwater, you'd already be half-dead," Will said. "Let's get ready. We'll have to hang our gunbelts around our necks and hold our rifles over our heads to try'n keep 'em dry while we're crossin'."

Both men took off their footwear and shucked off their gunbelts. Once their boots were hanging from their saddlehorns and the gunbelts in place around their necks, they remounted.

"We've got to come out on the other side where the bank ain't so steep, Jonas," Will said. "I know it's hard to tell, with the Pecos runnin' so high and fast, but that's the ford right in front of us. We're gonna have to ride upstream a ways before puttin' our horses into the river, since the current's gonna pull 'em downstream, so we'd never make it by goin' straight across."

Jonas shook his head.

"I dunno. That drop looks awful steep."

"It is, but just keep your horse's head high, and let him sit back on his haunches and slide down the bank. Once he hits the water, he'll start swimmin', whether he wants to or not."

"If you say so, Will. But if we don't make it, I just want to say I'm obliged for all you've done for me."

"*Por nada*. Don't talk like that, neither. We're gonna make it, then once we get to Austin, you can buy me a beer."

Despite his attempts to reassure Jonas, Will was just as afraid as the boy of this attempt. Horsehead Crossing was hazardous under the best conditions. Right now, it appeared downright deadly.

"If we survive today, I'll buy you two," Jonas said.

"You've got a deal," Will said. "Let's get movin'."

He lifted Pete's reins, clucked to the paint, and heeled him into a walk. They rode upriver for about a hundred yards. Will pulled his rifle from its boot, lifted it over his head, and nodded to Jonas. Jonas nodded in return, as he also pulled out his rifle and lifted it above his head.

Once Jonas was set, Will heeled Pete over the edge of the steep slope. Pete hesitated at the rim, snorted, tossed his head, then started down the bank. Will pulled back hard on the reins, keeping

Pete's head high as the horse half-ran, half-slid down the slippery sand and gravel riverbank. Pete plunged into the water, disappeared beneath the surface for a moment, leaving only Will's head, shoulders, and upraised arm visible, then bobbed back up. He began swimming strongly for the opposite shore.

At a splash behind him, Will turned in his saddle, to see that Jonas had also safely made the slide. He and Rebel were a few yards behind, Rebel fighting hard to keep from being sucked under and dragged downstream.

"Keep him headed as straight as you can," Will shouted to be heard over the rushing water. "If you miss the ford, there's no way out. You'll be carried away and drowned."

Jonas nodded, then took a tighter grip on his reins, shortening them to keep Rebel from turning and letting the current take him.

The crossing turned out to be even more hazardous than Will had expected. Several times, Pete nearly went under, and in one particularly rough stretch of water, was swept sideways several yards before Will could bring him around and again swimming for the eastern riverbank. However, the current finally slackened, the water shallowing as Pete neared the far shore. When his front hooves touched bottom, the paint lunged, trying to gain purchase, then scrambled out of the river. As soon as he did, Will tumbled from his saddle when a gunshot rang out. He rolled back into the Pecos.

"What the hell?" Jonas exclaimed, when he saw Will fall. He urged Rebel forward. As soon as the bay broke the water's surface, he took his lariat, shook it out, and built a loop. A bullet ripped the air alongside his head. Intent on saving Will at any cost, Jonas didn't take the time to return the hidden gunman's fire, instead whispering a hurried prayer that he, too, wouldn't catch a slug.

He ducked, then stayed low in the saddle as he sent Rebel pounding after Will, who was struggling weakly against the current as he tried to get back to the riverbank, apparently having taken a bullet, or else stunned in the fall from his horse.

"Hang on, Will!" Jonas yelled, as he swung the rope over his head. "I'll pull you outta there." He made his throw, which fell several feet short of the struggling Ranger. He cursed under his breath, knowing that he had just missed what was probably his only chance to save Will from the river's clutches. Desperately, he hauled the rope back out of the Pecos, seeing that Will was rapidly losing his fight against the raging water. He watched helplessly when the current pulled Will farther downstream. However, luck was with both men that day. Just when it appeared Will would be carried out of Jonas's reach, the current pulled him into a wildly swirling eddy.

"I'm gonna make another toss, Will," Jonas yelled. "Grab the rope."

He waited only a moment, until the current brought Will nearer the riverbank.

"Now, Will!" he shouted, then made his throw. This time, it was true. The loop settled around Will's upraised arm. As soon as Will grabbed the rope, Jonas took a dally around his saddlehorn. Being a trained cowpony, Rebel immediately began to back up, tightening the rope and pulling Will out of the river.

Jonas jumped off his horse and ran up to Will, who was lying on his belly, gasping like a beached fish. He rolled him onto his back.

"Will. You all right?"

"I—I dunno. Think so. Lemme get . . . my breath. Who was . . . shootin' . . . at us?"

"Dunno, but whoever it was seems to have stopped. Looks like you took a slug in your side. You're bleedin' pretty bad."

"Where's Pete? He didn't . . . drown, did he?"

"I don't know. He made it outta the river, but I don't know where he's at. I couldn't keep an eye on him while I was tryin' to pull you out. Lemme see how bad you're hit."

"Don't . . . worry about me . . . right now. You'd better . . . make certain whoever plugged me . . . ain't still hidin' in the rocks somewhere, with a gun trained on our backs. And try'n find Pete."

"Not until I'm sure you're okay," Jonas insisted.

"I'm all right. I'm startin' to get my air back," Will answered. "I need to know if Pete's safe. If you find him, there's bandages and salve in my saddlebags."

"Okay, but I hate leavin' you here," Jonas answered.

"Don't worry about me. Just find Pete. I have a sick feelin' the *hombre* who was shootin' at us wanted to steal our horses. Lucky for you I was in front, or that bullet would've had your name on it. Get goin', Jonas."

"I'm on my way. Be back in a few minutes. But what if I can't find Pete?"

"If you can't, and there's tracks, you trail him until you find the son of a bitch that stole him. Pete won't be able to go too fast or far, not after crossin' that flood."

"What do I do with the *hombre* when I catch up with him?"

"Plug him, if you have to," Will answered. "I don't care how. Nail him in the back, or from the front, whatever you need to do to stop him. Don't try'n get him to surrender, neither. Any man who'd shoot someone from ambush, then steal his horse, ain't gonna give himself up. Just don't let him get the drop on you. If that means shootin' him in the back, so be it."

"Understood."

Jonas caught up Rebel, mounted, and headed up the old stage road they were following. Once he was out of sight, Will closed his eyes and passed out. The next thing he was aware of was Jonas calling his name. He struggled to sit up.

"I'm right where you left me!" he yelled back. Once his vision came into focus, he could see Jonas approaching. Pete was trailing along behind him.

"I can see that," Jonas said, once he reached Will. He attempted a grin, but it came out as more of a flinch. He was clearly shaken. He nearly fell getting out of his saddle. "I found your horse, and I've already got the stuff from your saddlebags. Found a small bottle of whiskey in 'em, too. I figure you'll need that."

"What's wrong?" Will asked. "I can see you found Pete, but you look worse than I must . . . and I'm the one who caught a bullet."

"Yeah, I sure enough found your horse, a little way up the road," Jonas answered. "I also found the *hombre* who was shootin' at us, or more like what was left of him."

"Where?"

"Just beyond that mesquite thicket yonder," Jonas said. "He must've tried to ride your horse, but riled him somehow. Appears to me Pete threw him, then trampled him to death. There's hardly enough of whoever he was left for the buzzards. His head's all bashed in, his ribs are caved in, and his neck's busted. Just thinkin' about it has my stomach churnin' again."

"I should've warned you that you might find somethin' like that," Will said. "Pete's a good horse, and usually pretty gentle, but he doesn't take to rough handlin'. It's happened before with Pete. An *hombre* stealin' a horse is usually in a mighty big hurry, and doesn't much care how he treats the animal. Pete just won't tolerate bein' treated mean. Ain't that right, boy?" he said to Pete, who had wandered up to nuzzle Will's cheek.

"My guess is, the bastard who tried to kill me and take my horse must've lost his tryin' to cross the river. He waited to drygulch the first persons who came along, which just happened to be us. When he tried to ride my horse, Pete bucked him off, then stomped him. I reckon that son of a bitch won't ever try'n steal another horse."

"Not on this side of Hell, anyway," Jonas answered. "Will, you look like you're gettin' a bad chill. You'd better peel off those wet duds. I'll gather some driftwood and build a fire. Then I've gotta try and stop that bleedin'. You gonna be able to get outta your clothes?"

Will had started shivering, and his teeth were chattering.

"I'll . . . I'll manage." He winced when he tried to lift his gunbelt over his head, and pain shot through his ribs. "Just gimme a hand gettin' this . . . damn gunbelt off, that's all. And while . . . you're gatherin' . . . that firewood, see if you can find my rifle . . . and hat. I must've lost 'em when that *hombre* . . . plugged me. Sure hope they didn't fall into the river."

"I'll take a quick look for 'em, but right now, I think it's more important to take care of that bullet hole in your side," Jonas answered. He pulled the gunbelt off Will's shoulders and placed it alongside him. "The river's piled up plenty of wood. I'll only be a couple of minutes. You take it easy until I get back."

Will muttered something under his breath.

"Did you say somethin', Will?"

"Yeah. I said ain't no greenhorn kid gonna order me around."

"Suit yourself, but if you don't let this 'greenhorn kid' take care of you, you just might bleed to death, Ranger," Jonas snapped. He turned his back on Will and stalked off.

"Damn son of a bitch of a snot-nosed boy," Will muttered. Nonetheless, he had enough presence of mind to realize Jonas was right. He was indeed chilled from his near-drowning in the Pecos, and was beginning to feel light-headed. While he waited for Jonas to return, he pulled off his soaked clothes, then laid back in the sun. He instantly fell asleep.

Will was awakened by Jonas shaking his shoulder. He felt much warmer than when he had drifted off. He could smell burning wood.

"Will, you still with me?"

"Yeah. Yeah, I guess I am," Will said.

"That's good. When I came back and saw you lyin' there, I was afraid you'd bled out. I've got a fire goin'. It should warm you up pretty quick. And I did find your rifle and hat. They're over by the horses. Now, it's more'n high time for you to get patched up."

Will shook his head, and gave Jonas a dubious look.

"You gonna be able to handle that? Without gettin' sick, I mean?"

"It ain't gonna be any worse'n castratin' a calf, or doctorin' a sick horse," Jonas answered. "Yeah, I got sick after shootin' Kyle, but he was my kin. As far as the bushwhacker, I'd never seen a man torn up so much. I'll be able to fix you up okay. Now shut up and lemme take a look at you."

Jonas performed a quick examination of Will's wound. The ambusher's bullet had torn a long gash in Will's right side, down low along his ribs.

"Seems like you got lucky," he said. "The slug ain't in you. Another inch or so to the left and it would've buried itself in your belly. All that needs to be done is clean it out and bandage you up. Won't take all that long." Jonas glanced at the scar along Will's right cheek, and another puckered and faded bullet scar high on the left side of Will's chest. "I can see you've taken a bullet or two before, so I imagine you know this is gonna hurt."

"Not as much as your jabberin', instead of gettin' at it," Will answered, grinning.

"All right. I get what you're sayin'," Jonas answered. "It wouldn't hurt to stitch that wound up, and I saw you have heavy thread and a good-sized needle in your saddlebag, but they're dirty from bein' dunked in the river. I could douse 'em with some whiskey, or I could just clean out the wound, then dress and bandage it. If it starts bleedin' again later, then I'll have to stitch it. Up to you."

"I'd rather take a chance on just bandagin' it for now," Will said.

"That would've been what I'd done, if I were in your place," Jonas said. "I'll pour some of your whiskey over it, then coat it with the ointment and bandage you up. The bandages you had were soaked, too, but the fire's dryin' 'em out right quick, along with your clothes. You want a slug of whiskey before I start?"

"That's not a bad idea. Take one for yourself, too."

"I reckon I will."

Jonas uncorked the bottle and held it to Will's lips. After Will took a good-sized swallow, Jonas took one for himself, then poured a large splash of the fiery liquid over Will's side. Will winced at the sting.

"You doin' okay?" Jonas asked.

"About as good as a man who's been plugged and half-drowned can be," Will answered.

"Good. I'll bandage you up, then start boilin' some coffee," Jonas said. "Good thing you had that and the bacon wrapped in oilcloth. And it's a lucky thing the waterhole was on the other side of the river, too, so our canteens are full."

"Some coffee does sound good," Will said.

Jonas finished treating Will's wound, then got the coffeepot, two tin mugs, and the coffee from Will's saddlebags.

"You just take it easy, Will," he said. "By the time the coffee's done, your clothes should be dry enough so you can get dressed, long as the chills are gone."

"They are," Will answered. "I need to get those duds back on, anyway. I'm startin' to fry under this sun, and I think I'm startin' to get burned in places a man should never get burned."

Jonas winced, then burst into laughter. Will glared at him.

"It ain't funny, kid," Will grumbled.

"I—I'm sorry, Will," Jonas said, once his laughter had subsided. "It just struck me as funny, that's all."

"If you think it's so funny, why don't you undress and see how it feels?" Will retorted.

"Me? Not a chance!" Jonas answered. "I'll get your clothes."

· · ·

A short while later, they were sitting alongside the fire drinking hot coffee and munching on a few pieces of hardtack that had been inside the oilskin, so were still edible.

"As soon as we're finished eatin', we're gonna be on our way again, Jonas," Will said.

"Are you certain, Will? You gonna be able to ride?"

"I've ridden in worse shape than this," Will answered. "We need to keep movin', since my instructions are to be in Austin as quick as I can. Besides, I don't know about you, but I don't hanker to spend the night here, with those horse skulls grinnin' down at us and the bushwhacker's body just over yonder."

"I'm sure glad to hear you say that." Jonas paused, and shuddered a bit. "I wasn't lookin' forward to spendin' a night here, either. Just the thought gives me the willies. Speakin' of that bushwhacker, just what are we gonna do with him?"

"There's nothin' we *can* do," Will said. He shrugged. "We ain't got a horse to tie him to, and we ain't got a shovel dig a grave and bury him. You say there ain't much left of him, right?"

"Not enough to tell who he was, that's for certain."

"Then before we ride out, I'll check his pockets to see if he might've carried somethin' that tells us who he was, but I doubt it," Will said. "After that, you can pile some rocks over him, or drag him to the river, dump him in, and let the Pecos have him. Personally, I'd leave him for the buzzards. Any son of a bitch who'd shoot a man from hidin', then try'n steal his horse, don't deserve more'n that, anyway."

"I sure ain't that worried about him," Jonas said. "And I don't much feel like seein' that corpse again. As long as you don't mind, I'll wait here for you, while you check it."

"That's fine with me," Will said. "And I have to apologize to you, for snappin' at you when you were tryin' to help me. I reckon I was half out of my head, between gettin' shot, then fightin' the river."

"*Por nada*," Jonas said. "Don't mention it. You've done a lot more for me."

"Still, I'm obliged," Will said. "You're beginnin' to make a habit out of savin' my sorry hide, kid. Keep this up and I may want to keep you as a pardner, permanent like."

"I could learn a lot from you, that's for sure," Jonas answered. "There's an awful lot I don't know about bein' a lawman. Matter of fact, I don't know *anythin'* about bein' a lawman."

"With all the renegades in Texas, you'll learn real fast."

"I reckon. Will, I'll clean up while you check the body, if that's okay. I'll have everythin' ready to put back in your saddlebags soon as you get back."

"That sounds like a plan. I'll get Pete, ride over there, then come back for you."

It took Will only a few minutes to check the dead man's clothes. As he suspected, the bushwhacker carried no identification, or if he had, it had been destroyed when he'd apparently lost his horse while crossing the Pecos, and had to swim for his life. There were a few yellowbacks in his hip pocket, stuck together and faded from being soaked in the river, and nothing else. Will headed back to where Jonas was waiting, already mounted.

"Well?" he said.

"Like I figured, he didn't have anythin' on him. I don't imagine anyone'll be wonderin' what happened to him, either. You ready to ride?"

"Yeah," Jonas said. "I put your gear in my saddlebags for now. Figured you wouldn't mind."

"Not since we're ridin' together, anyway," Will said. "Let's head for Austin."

He heeled Pete into a walk. Once the horses were warmed up, he'd pick up the pace to a mile-eating lope.

6

Except for the Texas summer heat and dust, the rest of Will and Jonas's journey to Austin was uneventful. They reached the capital city about four in the afternoon. Will detoured a bit, to take Jonas to the seven hundred seventy-five foot high summit of Mount Bonnell, which overlooked the city and the Colorado River flowing through it.

"There she is, Jonas, Austin. We'll be at Headquarters within half an hour. What do you think of her?"

"It's the biggest damn place I've ever seen, Will," Jonas answered. "Sure hope we get to look around a little."

"We might, but I wouldn't count on it," Will answered. "If Cap'n Hunter wanted me back in a hurry, that means he's got somethin' planned. We'll most likely be ridin' back out again, either tomorrow or the next day, at the latest. No point in waitin' to find out. Let's go."

He lifted Pete's reins, backed him away from the summit's overlook, and led Jonas back down the mountain. A short while later, they were in the heart of the city.

"Boy howdy, it sure is crowded," Jonas said, as they weaved their way around scores of pedestrians, riders, carriages, and heavy freight wagons. Everyone seemed to be in a rush.

"It's a busy city, that's for certain," Will said. "The streets are usually bustlin' until late at night. We'll be turnin' left at the next corner. Headquarters is a few blocks up Congress Avenue. You worried?"

"I'd be lyin' if I said I wasn't."

"I wouldn't fret too much. Cap'n Hudson's a good man. Just about any Ranger in the outfit would ride to Hell and back for him. He'll listen to your story, and give you a fair shake."

"But what if he won't sign me on?"

"Try not to think about that. And try not to show him you're nervous. You don't want him to think you don't have the guts to be a Ranger before he gets to know a bit about you, do you?"

"No, sir." Jonas shook his head.

They had turned the corner onto Congress Avenue.

"Then try'n keep calm. That's Headquarters up ahead. We'll be there in a minute."

Shortly, Will and Jonas had tied their horses to a much-chewed hitchrail in front of Texas Ranger Headquarters, and were walking down a long, paint chipped corridor.

"Cap'n Hunter's office is just ahead, Jonas," Will said.

"I reckoned there'd be more people about," Jonas answered.

"Not very often. Most of the men are out in the field, and this late in the afternoon, most of the clerks have left. Cap'n Hunter'll still be here, though. His wife died a few years ago, and his kids are grown and gone. Since Emily passed, he spends most of his time here. He's even got a bunk in the barracks."

A thick haze of smoke marked the doorway of Captain Hunter's office.

"Looks like the place is on fire!" Jonas exclaimed.

"Nah, it ain't," Will answered. "I forgot to mention that's the one thing about the cap'n most of us *don't* like. He's got a real fondness for cheap Mexican cigars. He's always puffin' on one. If you can get out of our meetin' without gaggin' or chokin', that'll prove right there you've got the stuff to be a Ranger. Let's go on in."

Will knocked on the door frame.

"C'mon in," a gruff voice answered.

Will stepped inside Hunter's office, followed by Jonas.

"Howdy, Cap'n," he said, and sketched an informal salute. The Texas Rangers weren't much on military style formalities or discipline.

"Howdy yourself, Will," Hunter answered, as he stood up and came from behind his desk to shake Will's hand. Hunter was in his early sixties, his thinning gray hair and good-sized paunch attesting to his age. But his deep blue eyes were as clear as ever, his mind as sharp. He could still outshoot most men with the Smith & Wesson American he wore on his right hip. " 'Bout time you got back. Who's that you've got with you?"

"This is Jonas Peterson. Sorry we took so long, but with the Texas and Pacific not runnin' past Abilene . . ."

"Too late to worry about it now." To Jonas he said, "I'm Captain Paul Hunter."

"It's a pleasure to meet you, Cap'n Hunter," Jonas said, extending his hand.

"You too, son. But I'm a mite puzzled. Will, what's this boy doin' here?"

"Jonas? He's gonna be your newest Ranger, Cap'n."

"What makes you think I need any more Rangers?"

"Because I've been gone for a few weeks. In that time, at least one man must've been gunned down, stabbed, scalped, killed in a fall from his horse, or just plain up and quit, that's why."

"Unfortunately, you're right. Three Rangers have died, and two quit, since you rode out, so the outfit's short-handed. But—and no offense meant, Jonas—you don't look old enough to enlist."

"No offense taken, Cap'n. But I *am* eighteen. Got the proof in my mother's Bible, out in my saddlebags."

"I've seen it. Jonas ain't lyin', Cap'n. He's eighteen," Will confirmed.

"Okay, I'll give you that he's eighteen," Hunter answered. "Exactly what makes you think the boy is qualified for the Rangers?"

"Well, for starters, he saved my life, not once, but twice." Will answered. "For another, the circuit judge over in Pecos ordered me to have him enlist in the Rangers."

"I think mebbe you'd better explain that, Will."

"It's a pretty long story, Cap'n. I reckon it'd be best if you read the judge's verdict in Jonas's trial, and the reasons for all of this."

He handed Hunter the folded sheaf of papers he had kept tucked under his left arm, until now.

"This is pretty thick," Hunter muttered. "You two might as well pour yourselves some coffee and pull up a chair. It's gonna take me a while to plow through all this. Will, I know you don't smoke, but would you like one of my cigars, Jonas?"

"No, thank you, sir," Jonas answered. "Cigars are a mite too strong for my taste. I never have taken up cigarettes, neither."

"Suit yourself. But I'm gonna have another one." Hunter discarded the extinguished stub of a cigar he held clamped between his teeth, then pull another from his shirt pocket, struck a match, and lit it. Once he had the cigar going, he plopped into his chair, put on his spectacles, unfolded the papers, and began to read.

It took Captain Hunter forty-five minutes to read Judge Huttwelker's file on Jonas's case. Several times, he paused to ask Will or Jonas a question. Finally, he dropped the last page on his desk, and leaned back in his chair. He took the cigar butt he held tightly in his teeth from his mouth, and stubbed it out in the already overflowing ashtray on his desk. He took yet another cigar and a match from his shirt pocket, struck the match alight on his belt buckle, then lit the cigar and got it going before he spoke.

"Will, you've come back with some tangled messes before, but this one tops any of 'em."

"I know, Cap'n."

"By all rights, this young man should be going to prison. On the other hand, I can see why you don't want him to. And, I agree. Jonas, prison is no place for you. If I rejected the judge's decision, and sent you to Huntsville, I'm almost certain you'd come out a hardened criminal . . . either that, or be killed behind those walls. If you *did* survive, I'm certain before too long, the Rangers would be after you for committing more crimes.

"In addition, there is plenty of precedent for a man quitting his criminal career and joining the Rangers. Some of the best men the Rangers have had were, at one time, on the other side of the law. Therefore, I am going to have you enlisted as a Texas Ranger. And let me say right now I appreciate what you did for Will, here."

"Thank you, Captain Hunter," Jonas said.

"Let me finish, before you think you're getting off easy," Hunter answered. "My clerk has already gone home for the day, so we'll have to do the paperwork in the morning. Now, I realize you probably think you've already seen how difficult the life of a Ranger can be, since you and Ranger Kirkpatrick first confronted each other. Believe me, what you've been through so far was just a pea shoot.

"Once you sign on, you'll be a target for every renegade in the state. There's lots of law-abidin' folks who aren't too fond of the Rangers, either. You're also gonna have another weight on your shoulders. You make one mistake, just one, no matter how small, and you'll be on your way to Huntsville. That means you're to listen to everything Ranger Kirkpatrick tells you, to obey his every order.

"You'll also have to keep your temper in check, no matter how much you might get riled by somebody hasslin' you, or the local law not bein' happy about the Rangers comin' in and takin' over. I won't even talk about the physical and mental exhaustion. So, as long as you're certain you can handle everythin' that's gonna be thrown at you, tomorrow you'll be a Texas Ranger."

"I can handle it," Jonas assured him. "Anythin's better'n spendin' years behind bars. I won't let you down. You either, Will."

"I'm sure you won't, or I wouldn't have allowed you to sign up," Hunter said.

"Now that Jonas's status is settled, where're we headed, Cap'n?" Will said. "I figure whatever you've got planned must be pretty urgent, since you wanted me back so quick."

"You're not goin' anywhere, except home, Will," Hunter answered.

"Home? What the hell do you mean, *home,* Cap'n? We pushed our horses to their limits rushin' back here, and you're sendin' me home? Tell me this is some kinda bad joke."

"It ain't, and watch your tone with me, Ranger," Hunter warned. "You've got a couple of weeks leave comin', and you're gonna take it. You're goin' home for your sister's wedding."

"Cap'n, you know when I joined the Rangers my family didn't want anythin' more to do with me. I ain't been back home since I left. I sure don't intend to head back there now."

"You will, Ranger, and that's an order. Your father wants you home for your sister's wedding, and you will be there," Hunter insisted. "You know your father has the governor's ear."

"He's got more'n just the governor's ear," Will

shot back. "He's got the governor by his horse chestnuts. And as far as I'm concerned, he can have the whole damn governor."

"You're bordering on insubordination, Ranger," Hunter warned. "I don't know much about your history with your family, and frankly, I don't care. All I know is your father talked to the governor, who talked to the adjutant general, who talked to me."

"They can all go to Hell," Will muttered.

"Mebbe they will, someday," Hunter answered. "In the meantime, they're my bosses. I like my job, and intend to hold onto it as long as I'm able. That means you'll swallow your damn pride, or anger, or whatever's eatin' at your insides, and go to that wedding. Hell, Will, don't you have any feelin's, at least for your sister? Think of her, if no one else. How will she feel if you're not there when she gets married?"

"Can't you just tell my father that you had to send me on an assignment down along the border? One that just couldn't wait?"

"I think you already know the answer to that."

"Yeah, I reckon I do. Damn. Seems like you're not givin' me a choice, Cap'n."

"You're wrong, Will. You *do* have a choice. You can either take the leave you've got comin' to you, go to your sister's wedding, then be back here in two weeks, ready to return to work. Or you can turn in your resignation, right now."

"I think *you* know the answer to *that*." Will shook his head in defeat. "I'll go, but only for Susie. Now, what exactly am I supposed to do with Jonas?"

"Take him with you," Hunter answered. "Not to the wedding, of course, unless when you get home your family invites him. You can teach him some of what he needs to know while you're ridin' home and back, and if you have time, while you're there. You're makin' the right decision, Will. You won't regret it."

"Uh-huh," Will said, clearly not convinced.

"You know I'm right. Families, as aggravatin' as they can be, should still stick together, unless things are so bad it's impossible. I don't think that's the case here, or your father would never have contacted the governor to make certain you were home for the wedding. Since you're already runnin' late, you'll need to pull out as soon as Jonas is sworn in tomorrow. Lucky there's still a few days until the ceremony."

"Yeah, *real* lucky," Will said. He stood up.

"C'mon, Jonas, we've gotta care for our horses, then I'll show you where we bunk. After that, I'm gonna give you your first lesson as a Ranger . . . how to get rip-roaring drunk. Let's go."

He didn't even wait for an answer, just stalked out of the office. Jonas sat there in confusion.

"Go ahead with him, Jonas," Hunter said. "Try'n keep him outta trouble. The way he's feelin', I have a hunch you'll have your hands full."

"Yessir, Cap'n. And thanks. I'm obliged for your faith in me."

"I only ask you make certain it's not misplaced."

"I will," Jonas answered. He jammed his hat on his head and hurried after Will.

7

Will and Jonas left Austin just after ten o'clock the next morning, after Jonas had officially been made a Texas Ranger. They had spent most of the previous night in the Silver Star Saloon, the unofficial Rangers' barroom in Austin, downing more whiskeys than was wise for any man.

They had stumbled into the Headquarters barracks well after two in the morning, collapsed across their bunks, and passed out. Now, despite being severely hung over, they had somehow managed to get the gear on their horses, gotten some needed supplies at the nearest store, and were riding west, both of them slumped over in their saddles, heads pounding, stomachs churning, and mouths dry as cotton. Jonas, who had never drunk so heavily before in his life, was particularly miserable.

"How long have we gotta ride, Will?" he asked.

"Three days," Will answered. "Home's a little more'n a hundred miles from here. It's a small town just about halfway between Fredericksburg and Kerrville, on the edge of the Hill Country. We'll head west for a ways, then cut southwest. After pushin' these horses so hard to reach Austin, I ain't in any particular hurry. Since we

119

got a late start and are travelin' slow today, we'll reach town late mornin' on Thursday."

"Plus, you don't really want to go home, anyway," Jonas answered.

"There is that," Will admitted. "Although Cap'n Hunter was right about one thing. My sister Susie's the only one who understood why I had to leave home and join the Rangers. I'd hate to hurt her by not bein' there for her special day."

"Yeah, you'd have regretted that for the rest of your life," Jonas answered. His stomach rumbled, and bile rose in his throat. He was barely able to keep from throwing up all over Rebel's withers, and his saddle. He groaned.

"Will, I need to ask you a favor."

"Sure, Jonas. What is it?"

"Can we keep the horses to a walk, or a slow, easy lope, until I'm feelin' a bit better? Guess I drank a bit too much last night. I don't think I could handle a trot."

"You drank too much?" Will said. "As if I didn't? You really think I want to be jouncin' along at a trot, gettin' my guts bounced right outta me? We're gonna keep at a steady walk, at least for the mornin'. After we stop to eat somethin', if we can keep it down, we'll pick up the pace this afternoon."

"I appreciate that, Will. I'm grateful. *Gracias*."

"Not as grateful as my own belly is. Man, that sun is bright. Sure ain't helpin' my headache.

120

There's a patch of live oaks up ahead. We'll stop there and rest in the shade for a while, then push on."

"There she is, just ahead. My home town," Will said, right around eleven o'clock the following Thursday. He pointed to a sign that marked the town limits.

"Kirkpatrick," Jonas read, aloud. "You mean the whole damn town is named after your family?"

"Yeah, well, my father, anyway," Will answered. He pulled out his badge and pinned it to his vest as they passed the sign. "He's a banker. He was first vice-president at the First National Bank of Austin, then struck out on his own. He founded this town, startin' with his own bank, and never looked back. One thing I've gotta give him, the man's a success. He's a natural-born money man."

Jonas read the signs on several businesses as they rode into town: "Kirkpatrick Mercantile", "Kirkpatrick Dry Goods", "Kirkpatrick Feed and Grain", "Kirkpatrick House Hotel", "Kirkpatrick Harness Shop", and more. Even the church was the "Kirkpatrick Community Christian Church". The largest building, a two-story yellow brick structure, was the Kirkpatrick State Bank. He finally gave a low whistle.

"Boy howdy, you weren't kiddin', Will," he

said. "Does your pa really own all these places?"

"Most of 'em," Will said, with a shrug. "The owners of the few he don't paid him to put his name on their shops. Hey, Cletus," he called to a man standing in front of the harness shop.

"Will! Well I'll be hanged," Cletus Mayfield answered. "The prodigal son returns at last. You plannin' on stickin' around long? Who've you got with you?"

"No longer'n I have to," Will answered. "Just for Susie's wedding. I'll be hittin' the trail soon as it's over. This here's my new ridin' pard, Jonas Peterson. Jonas, Cletus Mayfield. He owns the harness shop."

Mayfield nodded.

"Right pleased to make your acquaintance, Jonas."

"Same here," Jonas answered, touching two fingers to the brim of his hat.

"See you later, Cletus," Will said, as he put Pete into a trot.

"We're gonna stop at the marshal's office before goin' to my family's house, just to let him know we're in town," Will told Jonas.

A few minutes later, after allowing their horses a short drink from the trough in the town plaza, they reined up in front of the Kirkpatrick Marshal's Office. They dismounted, looped their horses' reins over the rail, and went inside. There were two men in the office, one wearing a marshal's star, the other a deputy's. They looked up when Will and Jonas came in.

"I don't believe my eyes," the marshal exclaimed. He hurried from behind his desk to pump Will's hand. "Will Kirkpatrick. I honestly didn't ever expect to see you darken my door again. Welcome home, boy."

"Howdy, Max," Will said. "Good to see you again, too. This here's my new ridin' pard, Jonas Peterson. Jonas, Marshal Max Spurr, and his deputy, Art Mason."

The three men shook hands. Spurr was about the same age as Will, in his twenties, with curly dark brown hair, brown eyes, and a slim build. Mason was also young, no more than twenty-five, with sandy hair and green eyes. He was very thin, and stood ramrod straight.

"You boys want a cup of coffee, or are you headin' right for home?" Spurr asked.

"I reckon I can take the time to have some coffee with an old friend," Will answered. "Just don't tell Jonas any tales about the stunts we pulled as boys, Max."

"Great. I'll pour some. And I sure won't repeat those stories. We'd both lose our badges if they ever got out."

"How's my family doin'?" Will asked, while Spurr got some mugs off the shelf and began filling them from the pot keeping warm on the stove.

"They're all just fine," Spurr answered. "Susan's all excited about the wedding, of course. Your mother's busy gettin' ready for it too, plus always bein' the town hostess. You know how she and the Kirkpatrick Ladies' Sewing Circle and Reading Society keep rein on this town."

"I sure do," Will said, with a rueful smile.

"Your brothers are workin' hard at the bank. Jerry's been courtin' Cynthia Wallace. I wouldn't be surprised if they get hitched before too much longer."

"How about my father?"

"You know him, Will." Spurr shook his head. "Doesn't care much about anythin', except his bank. I reckon I don't need to say more'n that. And of course he never forgave you for not goin' into the bankin' business with him."

"No, you sure don't," Will answered. "I'd hoped he would, in time, but I guess he'll never change. I'm the black sheep of the family."

"Baaaah," Mason said.

"Careful, Art," Spurr cautioned.

"It's all right," Will said. "Art's just funnin' me. Anything else new in town?"

"Well, let's see." Spurr ran a hand through his hair. "Molly Preston had twin girls . . ."

For the next half-hour, Spurr and Mason caught Will up on all the occurrences in Kirkpatrick, few as they were, which had happened during

Will's absence. Finally, Will drained the last of his coffee.

"Well, I guess I've spent enough time here, Max," he said. "I'd better get on over to the house before word reaches my folks I'm in town. You gonna be at the wedding?"

"I sure am. Just about the whole town'll be there."

"Because they wanna be, or because my father summoned them?"

"A little of both," Spurr admitted. "You're well aware no one in this town dares say no whcn your pa asks them for somethin'. At the same time, when your family does throw a party, they have nothin' but the best. Since your sister's weddin'll be the biggest affair this town's ever seen, it should be some time. Most folks are lookin' forward to eatin' and drinkin' real good come Saturday. I know me and mine sure are."

"Even me'n Dolly are invited," Mason added. "Our kids, too. Lily's just a baby, but we were told she's welcome."

"Then if I don't run into you boys around town, I'll see you there," Will answered. "C'mon, Jonas, let's go. Time for you to meet my family."

"See ya later, Will, Jonas," Mason said. "Try'n stay out of trouble."

"I always do," Will answered.

"Yeah, right. *Sure* you do," Spurr muttered,

under his breath. "*Adios, amigos*," he added, loud enough to be heard.

Will and Jonas retrieved their horses, mounted, and made the short ride to Will's family's home, which was a large, two-story native limestone mansion, surrounded on three sides by a wide porch. Potted flowers and plants hung from the porch ceiling, and rocking chairs seemed to extend an invitation to visitors to sit and relax. The house was situated on a rise at the north end of town, from where it commanded a view of all of Kirkpatrick. When he first saw the house, Jonas yanked Rebel to a halt. He sat in his saddle, staring at the magnificent structure.

"*This* is where you grew up?" he exclaimed.

"Yup," Will said.

"And you left all this to be a Ranger, gettin' paid thirty a month and found, sleepin' on the hard ground, eatin' lousy grub, and gettin' shot at, with a horse your best friend?"

"Yup again. And I've never regretted it."

Jonas shook his head.

"I purely can't figure you, Will Kirkpatrick."

"Mebbe you'll understand a bit more about me before we leave this town," Will said. "C'mon, no point in puttin' this off." He walked Pete the short distance to the house, then he and Jonas dismounted and tied their mounts to two of the four black wrought iron horsehead hitching posts in front of the house. Will heaved a sigh as they walked up the brick sidewalk, another when they climbed the stairs and crossed the porch.

"We'll have to take our spurs off, Jonas," he said, reaching down to unbuckle the left one from his boot. "Can't have 'em cuttin' up the rugs, or gougin' the floors."

"You sure we won't have to take off every blamed thing we're wearin'?" Jonas asked, only half-kiddingly.

"Don't give my mother any ideas," Will cautioned. He unbuckled his other spur, then dropped them to the porch floor, as did Jonas with his. Once that was done, Will lifted the iron ring door knocker and rapped it against the heavy oak door, three times. A moment later, a face appeared in the door's leaded glass window, then it opened, answered by a young, red-haired green-eyed Irish woman, who wore a maid's uniform.

"Master William. You're home. Miss Susan will be so pleased you came back for her wedding."

"Peggy, I've told you over and over again I'm not *Master William,* just plain Will."

"Sure, and ye want me to lose me job," Peggy retorted. "The mister or missus would toss me out on me bum if they ever heard me not addressing ye as *Master William.* I see ye've brought a friend home with ye . . . and a very handsome one too, he is. Will ye introduce me, already?"

Her green eyes took on a devilish glint.

127

"Of course," Will said. "This is my new riding pardner, Jonas Peterson. Jonas, Margaret O'Connell, known to all of us as Peggy. She's been with the family for quite a few years now. I don't know how my mother would ever manage the house without Peggy, and Delia, the cook."

"Aye, and don't be makin' me sound like an ancient old maid in front of your friend, Master William," Peggy said.

"I sure wouldn't think of you as *old,* Peggy," Jonas said. "I'd say you're not a day over twenty."

"Aye, handsome he be, Will, and a flatterer, too. Ye'll be turnin' a lady's head with such sweet talk, Mister Jonas. I'll have you know I'm all of twenty-three years old. I came to America from Ireland when I was a mere slip of a lass. I've been employed by the Kirkpatricks since I was fifteen."

"You certainly are a sight for trail-weary eyes, Peggy. You must call me Jonas. I insist."

Peggy blushed almost as red as her flaming hair.

"Are ye certain ye don't have any Irish in ye, Jonas, me lad? Ye sure have the gift of the gab, like ye'd kissed the Blarney Stone."

Jonas shook his head.

"No, but after meetin' you, I purely wish I did."

"Peggy, are you gonna let us in the house, or

are you and Jonas just gonna stand here makin' sweet talk all day long?" Will said.

"Of course, of course. I don't know why ye think I have to let ye in, Master William. This is your home. Your old room is still exactly like it was when ye rode away."

"You mean it *was* my home," Will answered. "My father made it very plain it was no longer my home the day I left."

"Aye, that's all water under the dam, I mean over the dam, under the bridge," Peggy said. "He'll be glad to see ye. Step inside, now."

"Peggy, who's at the door?" a woman's voice called from the parlor.

"It's Master William, come home for the wedding, Mrs. Kirkpatrick," Peggy answered.

"William? William's here?"

There was a rustle of skirts, then a woman who was an older, shorter, female version of Will rushed into the hallway and raced up to him.

"William. You came home!" she exclaimed, as she threw herself into his arms to hug him. "I never thought I'd see you again. I'm so happy, and Susan will be thrilled. Let me look at you."

She took two steps back, and studied Will critically.

"You look horrible," she said, clapping her hands to her cheeks. "You're thin as a rail. You're filthy, you smell of horse and sweat. And that scraggly beard, and your hair. What's this?" she asked, touching the bullet scar on his right cheek.

"It's from a bullet," Will answered. "I had a bit of a close call down in Llano."

"Your father and I warned you that you'd be killed or crippled if you became a lawman. Well, you're home now. I'm certainly glad you came to your senses and quit roaming about for the Rangers. Don't you dare step anywhere else in this house until you've cleaned up. Head straight for the kitchen and tell Delia to draw you a nice, hot bath."

"Mother, I ain't quit the Rangers," Will said softly.

"What do you mean, you haven't quit the Rangers?" his mother said. "Please use proper English. You've had enough schooling to know how to speak properly." For the first time, she seemed to notice Jonas. "And just who is this . . . this saddle tramp you brought home with you?"

"Mother, don't start right in by insulting my friend," Will answered. "As I've just told you, I haven't left the Rangers. I came home for Susan's wedding, that's all. As soon as that's over, I'll be riding back to Austin for new orders. My friend ain't—*isn't*—a saddle tramp at all. His name is Jonas Peterson, and he's my riding pardner. The reason we're both so . . . unkempt . . . is because we rode like heck all the way from Pecos to here, at Father's summons. The Texas and Pacific tracks are washed out in several spots east of

130

Pecos, so we had to make the trip by horseback. Jonas, my mother, Claudette Roubideaux Kirkpatrick."

"Please do forgive me, Mr. Peterson," Claudette said. "It's just that William has been dragging all sorts of creatures in here ever since he was a little boy. One time, he even brought home a Negro child. Needless to say, we made certain *that* never happened again. Welcome to our home."

"There was no offense taken, Mrs. Kirkpatrick," Jonas said, as he took her proffered hand. "I realize I must look like somethin' the cat dragged in . . . or Will did."

Will rolled his eyes. His mother gave a slight laugh.

"Thank you for understanding. William, kindly take your guest to the kitchen, and tell Delia she'll need to draw *two* baths."

"That won't be necessary, Mother. We'll be going to Shalem's shop first thing in the morning for haircuts, shaves, and baths. We would have stopped there first, but as you know, he's closed on Thursdays. We need to tend to our horses, then we'll go upstairs to my room. Peggy, if you wouldn't mind, could you ask Delia to send some hot water, towels, and soap to my room, in about an hour. Pete and Rebel have been ridden hard for the past weeks, so I want to make certain they have a good feedin' and curryin' before me'n Jonas take care of ourselves."

"Of course, Master William."

"You really don't intend to traipse through the house in those filthy clothes, do you?" Claudette asked. "And those muddy boots will ruin the rugs. You know those came all the way from Persia."

"Don't worry, Mother. We'll use the back stairs. We'll also take off our boots before we come in. Unless you'd prefer we shed our clothes out on the porch."

"William!" Claudette shrieked. "How dare you talk like that when there are ladies present? I should have Delia wash out your mouth with soap."

"I think I'm a little too old for that, Mother. Before we take the horses around to the stable, is Susan home?"

"No, she is not," Claudette answered. "She's at the dressmaker's for the final fitting of her gown. It came from the finest shop in New Orleans, of course, but it was a bit too large, so Addie Hawthorne is taking it in. Everyone is so busy preparing for the wedding. Your Uncle Henri and Aunt Marguerite are here from Baton Rouge, your Uncle Martin and Aunt Louise came all the way from Memphis, and your Uncle Samuel and Aunt Martha are here from Kansas City. We wanted them to stay here at the house, of course; however, they said we had too much going on already with Susan's wedding. They insisted on staying at the hotel, and taking their meals in town."

"How about Father? Or Gerard and Bertram?"

"They're still at the bank. They should be home around four o'clock, as usual. Oh, William, your father was sorely disappointed when you didn't go into the banking business with him. He'll be even more disappointed when he finds out you've come home, only to leave again."

"I doubt that," Will said. "Besides, he's got Gerard and Bertram to take over when he finally retires, not that I ever expect him to. Mother, I hate to be rude, but me'n Jonas . . ."

"Jonas *and I* . . ." she corrected.

"Jonas and I have come a long way, in a short time. We're plumb worn out, and so are our horses. As long as it's all right with you, we'll care for Pete and Rebel, then clean up and take a nap. We'll see you for dinner. It's still at seven, isn't it?"

"It is, as always. Do you have anything suitable to wear?"

"We've both got spare shirts and denims in our saddlebags," Will answered. "Socks and underwear, too."

"You know we always dress up for the evening meal, William."

"We've got clean neckerchiefs, too."

"You can't possibly think Father and I would allow you to come to the dinner table dressed in cowboy rags," Claudette answered. "All your clothes are still in your room. Choose from them, for both yourself and your friend. They'll be too large for him, but they'll have to do."

"Mother, the day I left this house, I swore I'd never wear boiled shirts, stiff collars, and ties that half-choked me to death ever again. Jonas and I will wash up, and our spare clothes are clean enough so we'll be presentable. Unless you'd rather we rode into town and had dinner at the café."

"Of course not," Claudette said. "Don't be ridiculous. However, I can't speak for your father."

"You let me handle Father," Will answered. "Now, we're gonna take care of our horses. They've stood out there in the hot sun long enough. We'll see you at dinner. C'mon, Jonas."

"Nice meeting you, Mrs. Kirkpatrick," Jonas said, before he followed Will back outside. Peggy closed the door behind him.

"Now you see why I left and joined the Rangers," Will said.

"Your mother's a bit rough, but I dunno if I'd have given up all this just because of her," Jonas answered.

"Oh, it's not just my mother," Will explained. "We usually get along pretty well—or, at least, tolerate each other. Wait until you meet my father."

Pete whickered at Will's approach.

"I know, boy, and I'm sorry," Will said. He patted the paint's shoulder, and stroked his muzzle. "You're gonna get rubbed down and fed, right now."

"The first six stalls on either side are for my father's, brothers', and sister's horses, then the two large bays are for father's carriages. I don't see any of them here, so that means my brothers must have gone into the bank on their own today. We'll put Pete and Rebel in the two stalls at the other end of the barn," Will said.

"This is where your family's horses live?" Jonas asked, as he looked around the stable, with its wide aisles, large stalls, and polished walls. "It's better'n any place I ever called home."

"Yeah, it's a bit fancy for a stable," Will conceded.

"Who takes care of it? It's the cleanest barn I've ever seen."

"My father has a stableman and driver, Jose Calderon. He lives in that small house out back of the barn. He's not here, because he'll have driven my father into town. This must be one of the days when Father's got other errands for Jose," Will explained. "Let's get our horses settled, so we can clean up ourselves and get some rest before dinner. The tack and feed rooms are the ones alongside the carriage bays."

"Pete doesn't have his own stall?" Jonas asked.

"No. I bought Pete just before I left and joined the Rangers," Will answered. "My father took one look at him and refused to let him even come on the property. He called him a spotted bastard, that wasn't even fit for dog food, let alone a saddle horse. He won't own anything but the finest blooded Kentucky stock. He doesn't care how smart a horse is, just how pretty."

"He won't make us take Pete and Rebel out of the barn once he gets home?"

"I dunno," Will admitted. "If he does, we'll just take 'em down to Buck's Livery Stable. Buck's a decent *hombre*, and he owns his place, not my father. I'd've left 'em with Buck already, but I'm too tired to walk from the other end of town up to this house."

It took Will and Jonas the better part of an hour to feed, water, and groom their horses. Once they were finished, they went back to the house, entering through the back door, and using the back stairs to reach Will's bedroom on the second floor.

8

"Boy howdy, I ain't never slept in a room like this," Jonas said, as he sat on the edge of Will's full-sized bed, and looked around the large, high-ceilinged room, with its palladium windows and sumptuous furnishings. "Never slept on a mattress this soft, neither."

"I wouldn't get used to it," Will answered, as he draped his saddlebags and gunbelt over the back of a ladder back chair alongside a walnut desk. "We won't be here all that long."

"Mebbe so, but I'll take advantage of the accommodations while we are," Jonas said. He started to lie back on the bed, then, remembering his sweaty, filthy clothes, thought better of it. He stood up, took off his gunbelt and hung it alongside Will's. He settled deeply into a brown leather chair. He pulled off his boots, stretched out his legs, and pulled his hat down over his eyes.

"Leave me be until supper, Will," he said.

"It's *dinner* in this house," Will said. "Someone's gonna have to wake us both up." He sat in the leather chair next to Jonas, and, like him, pulled off his boots, stretched out, and tugged his Stetson over his eyes. Both men were instantly asleep. A few minutes later, there was a soft knock at the bedroom door.

"Master William?" When there was no answer, the knock came again, harder, and the voice called a bit louder. "Master William?"

Will stirred. He mumbled sleepily.

"Who is it?"

"It's Delia. I've brought the things for you and your friend's baths."

"All right. C'mon in, Delia." Will reached over and shook Jonas's shoulder. "Wake up, pardner. Time to clean up."

The door opened, and Delia, the cook and other maid, came in. She was a black woman, of average height, slightly on the stout side but certainly not plump. Her black hair was cut short. She wore a maid's uniform identical to Peggy's, but with a longer skirt, and over the uniform a long, white cook's apron. She carried two pitchers of steaming hot water by their handles with her left hand, and a stack of towels and washcloths, as well as an extra basin, in her right.

"Master William, it's so good to see you home," she said, in a soft southern Louisiana accent. "This house is a lot less cheery without you about."

"I've missed you too, Delia," William said. He kissed her on the cheek. "I'd like you to meet my new riding pardner, Jonas Peterson. He's just joined the Rangers."

"It's a pleasure," Jonas said, nodding his head to her.

"It's always nice to meet a friend of Master William's," Delia said.

"Well, we didn't quite start out as friends, but that's changed," Jonas answered.

Delia gave Jonas a knowing look, but said nothing. She set the towels and pitchers on the washstand, then took two bars of Pears' soap from her apron pocket and placed them next to the towels.

"I'm sure you boys are more than ready for your washings," she said. "Master William, your sister will be so happy you came home for her wedding. She really didn't expect you, of course. I've got to get dinner started. We'll chat later."

"I wouldn't miss Susie's wedding for all the renegades in Texas," Will answered. "Thanks for the water and towels, Delia. Me'n Jonas'll see you at dinner."

"I'll see you then."

As soon as Delia closed the door behind her, Will and Jonas went over to the washstand.

"Will, I've been meanin' to tell you, and finally remembered. Thanks for not tellin' the sheriff or judge back in Pecos I'd tried to kill you," Jonas said. "If you had, I'd've been on my way to Huntsville for certain. I'm much obliged you didn't bring that up."

"I didn't think it was necessary," Will answered. "You were merely scared out of your wits. I might've done the same if the boot was on the other foot. Besides, we're even on that score."

"We are? How?" Jonas asked.

"You didn't tell Delia the real reason I came home . . . that I had no choice," Will explained.

"Like you just said about me, I didn't see any reason to," Jonas answered. "Boy howdy, that hot water's sure gonna feel good. Let's get to work."

Will and Jonas stood side by side at the wash stand. They removed their dirty socks and shirts, then tossed them on the floor. Each poured water from a pitcher into a basin, then took a washcloth and bar of soap, worked up a lather, and started washing their hair, then their faces, necks and upper torsos. Will had just ducked his head into the basin to rinse the soap out of his hair when the door to his room burst open.

"Will! You came home for my wedding!" his sister Susan shouted. She ran across the room. Will turned and caught her just as she flung herself at him. "Let me look at you."

"Susie! We're not decent," he exclaimed, as she grabbed him and spun him around. For his part, Jonas picked up his shirt and hastily pulled it on.

"I've seen you without a shirt on lots of times, big brother," Susan retorted. She glanced at Jonas, whose fingers fumbled in his attempts to button his shirt. "As far as being decent, your friend looks *quite* decent to me."

Jonas flushed bright red.

"Susie! You're engaged," Will said. "Plus if

140

Mother ever heard you talkin' like that, she'd have a conniption. And Father would disown you."

"Pshaw! I'm tired of Mother and her impossible standards. As far as Father, he wouldn't dare disown me. Not when I'm marrying the only son of the largest rancher in Gillespie and Kerr Counties. He'd be too afraid Harvey's father would pull his money out of the bank."

"Still, what if me'n Jonas didn't have our britches on when you burst in on us, unannounced?" Will answered.

"Then I'd have left immediately . . . after taking a good look at Jonas," Susan answered, a wicked smile crossing her face. "Now that your friend seems to have managed to button his shirt, are you going to introduce us?"

"I reckon I should," Will said. "Susan, this is my ridin' pardner, Jonas Peterson. Jonas, my sister Susan."

"Charmed, I'm sure, Mr. Peterson," she said, as Jonas took her hand.

"It's an honor to meet you, Miss Kirkpatrick," Jonas said.

"Please, call me Susan, or better still, Susie. Mother and Father hate it, but they've given up trying to change me. May I call you Jonas?"

"Of course."

"There, that's settled. Will, it's so good to see you again. When you rode off and joined the

Texas Rangers, I was certain you'd never come back home. Not that I'd blame you."

"I can see that you and your sister would like to talk, Will," Jonas said. "I think I'll go outside and wander around. Look this place over."

"That's not at all necessary," Susan said. "There's nothing my brother and I have to hide. I'm certain I can also count on your discretion, Jonas."

"You have my word."

"Fine." Susan turned her attention back to her brother. "Will, you're looking wonderful, all fit and tan . . . except for that awful scar on your cheek. You've put on a lot of muscle. You could never have done that working for Father."

"That's what comes from hard ridin' and fresh air," Will said. "But you know that's not the reason I left home. I could never stand workin' indoors, which was the only option I would have had if I'd stayed in this town. The scar came from a horse thief's bullet, who didn't want to give himself up when I tried to arrest him. He wasn't as lucky as me. I drilled him dead center."

"I have to admit, it does give you a certain, rugged *je ne sais quoi*," Susan said. "I would imagine the ladies find it quite attractive. Well, perhaps not the kind of ladies Mother would want you to associate with."

"Susie!" Will exclaimed again. To Jonas he

142

said, "You'll have to excuse my sister. She has always been a bit . . . unconventional."

"Go ahead and say it, Will. I'm a rebel," Susan answered. "The only reason I've been able to get away with so many things other girls can't is because I'm the only daughter, with three brothers."

"That, and ever since you turned fifteen you've been shamelessly throwin' yourself at Harve Prescott, who is both the social and financial catch of Gillespie County." Will answered. "If I didn't know you better, little sister, I'd say this is more of a business partnership between Father's bank and the Rocking P, than a marriage."

"You make me sound like a gold digging trollop, who is only interested in marrying for money," Susan protested. "I'll have you know Harvey and I are very much in love, William Howard Kirkpatrick."

"I'm glad to hear that," Will said. "I wish you and Harve nothin' but many years of happiness."

"Thank you. I must say, however, that if anyone in this family is the *true* rebel it's you, Will. Defying Mother and Father's wishes by running off and joining the Texas Rangers, rather than going to work at Father's bank, and eventually taking over as its president."

"I would have suffocated being behind a desk keeping track of figures all day long, Susie," Will answered. "Plus I'd never have gotten out from under Father's thumb. Joining the Rangers is the best thing I've ever done. It's the life I've always wanted, the one I chose, and I live it. I'm helpin' make Texas safer for honest folks. It's just a shame I'll never be able to make our parents understand that. Besides, Father has Jerry and Bert to take over the bank. They're both more than happy to be bankers. He doesn't need me."

"As long as you're happy."

"I am. Very happy. Of course, Father will never understand. Mother either. Listen, Susie, me'n Jonas rode a long way in a short time to get here, and we're plumb tuckered out. Do you mind if we finish washin' up so we can get some shut-eye before dinner? We'll have plenty of time to talk later, or tomorrow."

"Certainly, Will. I apologize. I should have realized you'd be exhausted after your journey. Has Mother heard you speaking like a cowboy yet?"

"A little," Will admitted. "She wasn't too pleased about it."

"I would imagine she wasn't," Susan said, with a laugh. "Jonas, before I leave, would you like me to wash your back? I can reach the spots you can't."

"Susie!" Will said. "And *you're* worried about Mother hearin' *me* talkin' like a cowhand? If she ever heard you . . ."

"She'd be scandalized, and probably faint dead

away," Susan finished for him. "Jonas? My offer still stands."

"That won't be necessary," Jonas answered. "I do thank you, however."

"Handsome, and gallant," Susan said. "Perhaps I should run off and join the Rangers. All those attractive men . . ."

"You try that and I'll tan your bottom myself, little sister," Will said.

"I dare you to try it," Susan answered. "You needn't worry. Living on the Rocking P with Harvey will be more than enough of the rancher's life for me. I'm leaving now. I'll see you both at dinner. Will you be dressing for it?"

"In clean range clothes," Will answered.

"That should give Father apoplexy. I wasn't very hungry, but now I wouldn't miss dinner for the world. Nice meeting you, Jonas. You *will* be coming to my wedding, of course."

"If you'd like that."

"Of course I'd like that. In addition, it would be incredibly rude not to invite Will's friend to the wedding . . . no matter what Mother, Father, and my other brothers think. There's nothing like a bit of scandal to liven up a special day, and your being there will give the ladies of Kirkpatrick something to gossip about for weeks. Goodbye, for now."

Susan flounced out the door and slammed it behind her.

"Boy howdy, your sister is sure somethin', Will," Jonas said. "She looks a lot like you, too. I'll bet she'll be a handful for her new husband."

"She sure is, and she sure will be. But Harve Prescott's a real fine feller. I'd rather see Susie marry him than just about anyone else in these parts," Will said. "All of us kids pretty much take after my mother, at least as far as looks go. Let's finish cleanin' up and get that sleep. We'll be summoned downstairs before six-thirty. My father insists the family gather before dinner for drinks."

The knock on Will's door came even earlier than he expected.

"Master Will, your brothers are waiting for you in the library," Peggy said, through the closed door. "They'd like to talk with you before your father does."

"Tell them I'll be down in fifteen minutes, Peggy," Will answered. "Thank you."

"Of course."

Peggy's call had also awakened Jonas.

"Suppertime already?" he asked, still groggy from sleep.

"Not quite," Will replied. "My brothers want to talk with me before he does. I wonder what about."

"Only way you'll find out is to go talk to them," Jonas pointed out.

"You're right. Let's get dressed and get down there."

"You want me with you?"

"Yep. Just in case things get ugly and I end up headin' into town."

The two men put on clean underwear, socks, shirts, and neckerchiefs. They beat the dust out of their denims and hats, and brushed off their boots as best as possible. Jonas raised an eyebrow when Will buckled on his gunbelt.

"You expectin' to have a gunfight with your brothers?"

"Not a chance," Will answered. "They don't ever go armed. But a lawman just don't feel comfortable unless he's wearin' his sidearm. You'll figure that out, in time."

Jonas shrugged, then put on his own gunbelt. He followed Will down the stairs, through the parlor, and into the walnut-paneled library. Two younger, and paler, versions of Will were standing alongside a heavy cherrywood sideboard. One of them closed the door.

"Will," the older of the two said, "I see you've decided to come back home." The look on his face indicated he was far from pleased to see his brother.

"Yeah, what brought you back?" the other man said. "Did you run out of money, so you came running the hell home, looking for a handout?"

"No 'howdy'?" Will answered. "Not even a

damn introduction for my *amigo*? What's the matter, boys?"

"*You're* what's the matter, Will," the first brother answered.

"Jonas, I can see my brothers ain't gonna get around to introducin' themselves," Will said. "The older one is Gerard. The one who's already holdin' a drink is Bertram."

"Will's a good friend," Jonas said. "It's an honor to be able to meet his family."

He held out his hand, which Will's brothers shook, perfunctorily.

"It's kind of welcome to see Will found a friend who's like him," Bert said. "A damn no-good drifter."

"A damn no-good drifter who's now come back to take over the family bank, after me and Bert spent the past two years helpin' our father build it into the most powerful financial institution in Kerr and Gillespie Counties," Jerry added.

"Listen, let's get things straightened out right now," Will said. His face was dark with anger. "I came home for Susie's wedding, and that's all. In fact, the *only* reason I'm here is because Father put pressure on my commandin' officer to force me to show up. When I had a chance to think on it, I'm glad I did. I wouldn't have wanted to hurt Susie. Just as soon as the weddin's over, me'n Jonas are goin' straight back to Austin. I've got no intention of ever quittin' the Rangers. Now, is one of you at least gonna offer us a drink?"

"You know where the liquor is, right in front of you," Jerry said. "If you want a drink, pour yourself one."

"I reckon I'll do just that." Will picked up a cut crystal decanter from a tray on the sideboard, and filled two cut crystal glasses brim full. He passed one to Jonas.

"To my brothers," he said, lifting the glass. "Who are so very happy to see me return."

He downed the glass's contents in one swallow.

Jonas retreated to a corner of the room, where he sipped his drink. He wanted no part of this family disagreement. It was none of his affair.

"Will, why exactly did you come back?" Bert repeated. "You made it plain when you left you no longer wanted any part of this family."

"I did no such thing," Will answered. "I told Father I had no desire to spend my life as a banker, sittin' behind a desk, countin' money, keepin' track of figures, and foreclosin' on folks who, through no fault of their own, fell on hard times, because of drought, floods, blizzards, or just plain bad luck. When I said I wanted to strike out on my own and become a lawman, he told me in no uncertain terms I was no longer welcome here, and might as well forget I had a family. 'You can go straight to Hell, for all I care', were his exact words. Mother pleaded with me to stay, but she finally gave in.

"I'm not the one who wanted to cut ties . . . they did. You two were also pretty damn happy when I left, since that meant you'd both move up in the bank faster. For some reason, y'all seem to think I'm angry about that. Nothin' could be further from the truth. I love bein' a Ranger, and I'll stay a Ranger as long as I can sit a horse and fire a gun. Susie's the only one who understood that, and who said I was doin' the right thing when I left home.

"Bert, like I just said, I came home for Susie's wedding, plain and simple. Me'n Jonas'll be headin' back to Austin Sunday or Monday. I'd like to leave here on good terms with my family. It's up to you all whether that happens or not."

Will poured himself another drink. The room fell into an awkward silence. Jonas pretended to be deeply engrossed in studying the books on the shelves, and the family portraits on one wall. He turned when the door opened, and a man, clearly Will's father, came into the room.

While Will did not resemble his father nearly as closely as him mother, the relationship was still obvious. He had Will's build, except age had given him a slight paunch, and silver tinged the hair at his temples. He wore a full, salt-and-pepper beard, and was dressed in an expensive businessman's suit. A gold chain was draped across his middle, one end going into his vest pocket, where it was attached to a heavy turnip watch. A wedding band was on his left ring finger, and a large diamond ring on his right. He walked straight to the sideboard and poured himself a sherry.

"William," he said, after downing most of his drink. "You came home, after all. I half expected you to ignore my summons. You always were an obstreperous child."

"I would have ignored your *demands,* Father, except you got to Cap'n Hunter, and left neither one of us a choice," Will answered. "Despite that, I still wouldn't have come home if it weren't for Susie. She stood up for me when no one else would. I damn sure wouldn't want to hurt her by not attending her wedding."

"I assume that means you still haven't shown the intelligence God gave you, quit the Rangers, and come back to work in the bank."

"The intelligence God gave me *is* the reason I joined the Rangers. I didn't want to spend my life under your thumb, doin' a job I hated. It's not like you didn't have Jerry and Bert."

"Gerard and Bertram. They've outgrown child-hood nicknames, just like you. I know that they stayed with me, and I'm grateful to them. Still, the oldest son's place is working in the family business, and taking it over when the time comes. You haven't been home to learn this, of course, but I intend to run for State Senator come the next election. How will it look, if my firstborn son is doing a common lawman's job, chasing criminals, rather than pursuing a *real* career? What will I tell the voters?"

"You might try the truth," Will said. "Tell them I'm doing what I want, and that I'm helping rid Texas of the dangerous element so common in this state, so it will be safer for honest folks. My bein' a Ranger is no reflection on this family. It's not like I'm out robbin' trains or rustlin' cattle."

"It's below your social station."

"That's what's always been the most important thing for you, hasn't it, Father? Money and position. I'd bet my hat State Senator is just the start for you. You won't be satisfied until you're elected Governor, or maybe United States Senator. If that's what you want, I hope you succeed. But you'll have to satisfy your political ambitions without me. I'm happy with my life, I'm helping people, and I intend to remain a Ranger as long as I can ride a horse and shoot a gun."

"I see. Then, there's nothing further to discuss, is there?"

"Not as far as I'm concerned," Will answered. "You, Mother, Susie, Jerry, and Bert are my family, and I still care deeply about all of you, whether or not you choose to believe that. Whether you all care to reciprocate is up to you. But I'm gonna live my life as I damn well please, no matter what."

"Don't expect me to give you any money, if you run short," his father warned.

"I don't want any if your damn money," Will answered. "I don't need a lot, just my horse, gun, and food. Also, a good pardner to watch my back. You haven't asked me yet, so I'll introduce you to my ridin' pard now, Jonas Peterson. Jonas, as I'm certain you've figured out, this is my father, Silas Kirkpatrick."

"I'm honored to meet you, Mr. Kirkpatrick, sir," Jonas said.

"Don't try'n fool me, boy," Silas said. "You've been here for the entire conversation. I do have to thank you for bcing so gracious during this unpleasant scene."

"You're welcome, sir."

Silas pulled the watch from his vest pocket, and checked the time.

"I'm sorry to say I was detained at the bank by a client, so we won't have time for another drink before dinner. William, you and your friend haven't dressed yet."

"We've cleaned up as best we can, Father. Rangers don't exactly carry fancy duds around in their saddlebags. Mother is already aware that these are the best we've got."

"Well, then I guess they'll have to do, but only because I don't want to upset Susan," Silas answered. "Otherwise, I'd throw you both out on your rears. You remind me of the parable about

153

the wedding guests who showed up not properly dressed for the feast. This is the first and last time you'll ever eat in this house without being correctly attired. Let's go into the dining room for our meal."

9

Will's mother and sister were already seated at the elaborately carved walnut dining table, one on each side. His father kissed them both on the cheek, then sat at the head of the table. Jerry sat next to his mother, Bert his sister. That left Will and Jonas the two opposite chairs at the lower end of the table, which was covered with a dazzlingly white linen tablecloth. It was set with fine bone china, decorated in a delicate pink floral pattern, sterling silver flatware, and etched crystal glasses.

"I know as the oldest, your place was next to your mother, William," Silas said, "However, you forfeited that when you left home."

"It doesn't matter where I sit," Will answered. "You can just treat me as a guest, one who you aren't necessarily happy to have here, but etiquette dictates must be invited, and treated decently."

He and Jonas removed their hats and sat down.

"Please, might we have no unpleasantries, at least during our meal?" Claudette said.

"Thank you, Mother," Susan said. "I was about to make the same request."

Claudette picked up a small silver bell from alongside her salad plate and tinkled it. Peggy came through the kitchen door.

"Are you ready to begin dinner, Mrs. Kirk-patrick?" she asked.

"Yes, Peggy. You may begin to serve."

"Very good, ma'am."

Peggy went back into the kitchen, and returned a moment later with a tureen of vegetable soup. She filled everyone's bowls.

"We never eat before saying Grace," Silas said. "Susan, since this will be one of your last nights home before your wedding, would you kindly lead us in the prayer?"

"Of course, Father," she answered. "Everyone, please bow your heads."

Once everyone's heads were bowed, and hands folded in prayer, she gave the blessing.

"We thank Thee, O Lord Almighty God, for the health of our family, and for the bountiful food You provide, especially that of which we are about to partake. We also thank You for the safe return of our brother and son, William, and for the company of his guest, Jonas. We humbly ask You to bless this table, this family, and to keep us safe, especially William and Jonas in their careers as peace officers. We offer Thee thanks, Lord, for all Your blessings. Amen."

"Amen."

"We may now begin to dine," Claudette said.

"Gerard, would you pass me the butter?" Bert asked, as he took a slice of bread from a plate, then passed the plate to Susan.

· · ·

The meal ran for seven courses and over two hours. It was after nine o'clock when it finally concluded.

"Susan and I are going into the parlor to finish the needlepoint sampler we've been working on, while you men go into the library for your cigars and after-dinner drinks," Claudette said. "Just don't linger too long over them. Tomorrow will be a busy day for all of us, with the wedding on Saturday."

"Come with us, William, Jonas," Silas ordered. He led the other men back to the library.

"George at the tobacco shop just received a new shipment of expensive cigars, and he set several aside for me," he said, once they were back in the room and the door closed. "They are hand-rolled, with the wrapper being broad-leafed tobacco grown in the Connecticut River Valley of New England." He picked up a rosewood humidor from his desk and opened it.

"Please, take one," he said.

Bert and Jerry each chose a cigar. Will shook his head.

"I'm sorry, Father, but I still haven't taken up smoking. You know I've never enjoyed it."

"Another way you're different from your brothers and me," Silas said. "Mr. Peterson?"

"I haven't smoked much either, but I'll give

one a try. Thank you," Jonas said. He took a cigar from the box, as did Silas.

"Before we light up, I'll pour us all a cognac," Silas said. "I have several bottles of Remy Martin VSOP, which is shipped specially for me all the way from France. William, I know you won't refuse that. You do enjoy a fine liquor."

"You're right, Father, and that's one thing I still miss about home. You certainly can't get a good brandy or scotch in any frontier saloon. It's almost always cheap rotgut."

"Crudely put; however, I'm certain you're correct in your assessment," Silas answered. "Just a moment, while I open the bottle and fill our glasses."

Silas removed a full bottle of Remy Martin from a cabinet, uncorked it, and poured generous amounts of it into five snifters.

"Mr. Peterson, I doubt you've ever experienced a fine cognac such as this before," he said, as he handed Jonas one of the glasses. "You hold the glass with the bottom in the palm of your hand, and gently swirl the contents. The warmth of your hand and the swirling releases the aroma of the liquor, and allows the flavors to fully emerge. To properly enjoy it, you should take a sniff before you take your first sip. It will be a true delight to your palate, I assure you."

"What my father is tryin' to tell you, Jonas, is you don't just gulp this stuff down in one quick swallow," Will said. "You drink it slowly, letting it sit on your tongue. Drinking it slowly allows you to truly appreciate it."

"You haven't lost your entire sense of social graces after all, William," his father said. "I'm glad to see you still have *some* of the family's good taste."

"It's not because I haven't tried," Will answered, smiling.

"That's not at all humorous," his father answered.

"Coming from my brother, I thought it was," Bert mumbled. "Then again, perhaps not," he said, any thought of disagreeing with his father withering under Silas's glare.

After two cognacs each, Will decided he'd had enough for one night.

"Father, I know you expect the entire family to be in bed by eleven o'clock," he said. "However, I'm gonna take Jonas into town and see if I can round up some of my old friends for a couple of drinks."

"I should have known," his father answered. "You're not even home a day and you're ready to run off and find the rowdy bunch you ran with. That riff-raff is what started you on the road to perdition."

"I'd hardly call joining the Texas Rangers going to Hell," Will answered. "Listen, Father,

I came home only because you didn't leave me any choice . . . my captain made that very clear. That, and I realized I didn't want to hurt Susan. She's the only one who understood why I had to get out of this house, this town. I'm only going to be here for the wedding, then I'll be gone. For Susan's sake, can we at least try to be civil while I'm here?"

Silas hesitated before replying. "I'll do my best. However, I am still deeply angry over your abandoning everything I have built for my children. You could have had wealth, power, and social standing, William. You still can, if you'll apologize, resign from the Rangers, and come back home."

"You still don't understand, and you never will. I don't want any of those things that are so important to you, Father. I have to do what I want to do, what I enjoy. I love being a lawman, love the freedom of being on horseback, riding through the badlands, depending on no one but myself, my horse, and my pardners."

"*Partners.* You're even speaking like a common range rider."

"Pardners. Yes, I am. I don't have to act like some high-falutin' dude, either. And you'll still have Jerry, Bert, and Susan to carry on your legacy."

"Gerard and Bertram. And just to keep the record clear, the only reason I insisted you come home for the wedding was because your sister and mother hounded me until I gave in. Bringing you back was *their* idea. So was allowing you to sleep in your old room. Had it been up to me, you would have stayed at the hotel, or Widow Jackson's boarding house."

"Where I would have been perfectly happy," Will answered. He glanced at the mantel clock. "I don't want to keep you past your bedtime. Perhaps me'n Jonas will see you at breakfast, but I doubt it. I intend to sleep in, then we're going to Shalem's to get haircuts, shaves and baths. We probably won't be home until just before dinnertime."

"Suit yourself. Just don't come running back to me when you get tired of being broke and hungry. The door will be closed."

"You made that plain the day I left home, Father. C'mon, Jonas, let's get outta here."

"*Now* I really understand why you left home," Jonas said, as he and Will rode into town. "Boy howdy, I'd suffocate in that damn house. No amount of money would make livin' here worthwhile. No offense meant."

"None taken. I was bein' smothered here," Will answered. "Everythin' we kids did had to be just perfect, to make certain it would be 'proper' in the circles my mother and father associate with."

"What're your folks' backgrounds, if you don't mind my askin'?"

"Not at all. My father is one of a long line of financiers from back East. The family history claims that one of his ancestors even helped fund troops for the American Revolution. My grandfather moved to Texas, and founded the First National Bank in Austin. When he passed away, my father took his inheritance and started his own bank, and, of course, town. I will give him this much. My father's an absolute genius when it comes to makin' money."

"That's pretty obvious. What about your mother?"

"She was a high society ingénue, a French lady from New Orleans. My father met her when he was down there on a trip. Her family was old New Orleans stock, but they'd pretty much gone busted. They were livin' in a run-down, termite and rat infested mansion, tryin' to act as if they still had power and influence. My father had money, my mother's family needed it, so it was a perfect match. And they do love each other, although they don't often show it."

"Of course, the money helps."

"For them, yeah. They both worship it. That, and status, particularly for my mother. She's never forgotten her family was once the crème de la crème of New Orleans society. Damn it, there I go. Sometimes I still sound like 'em. Anyway, enough about my family. There's the saloon, just ahead. I'm gonna have me a few whiskeys and try to forget about my family for the rest of the night. C'mon, Pete."

He put his paint into a trot. A moment later, he and Jonas reined their horses up in front of the Kirkpatrick Saloon. They dismounted, looped their reins over the rail, then climbed the stairs and pushed open the batwing doors. The bartender shouted a greeting as soon as they stepped inside.

"Will! I'd heard you were back in town, you son of a gun. 'Bout time you came 'round. Who's your friend?"

By the time Will and Jonas reached the bar, he'd already pulled a bottle of Old Granddad from the back bar shelf, uncorked it, and placed the bottle and two glasses on the mahogany.

"I had to go by the house and see the family first, Gordon," Will answered.

"I can imagine how that went," the bartender answered.

"Yup. Gordon, this here's Jonas Peterson. He's just signed on with the Rangers. He's my new ridin' pard. Jonas, meet Gordon Simon. He owns this place. He doesn't water down his drinks . . . too much, and his games are honest . . . sort of."

"Gee, thanks a lot, Will," Simon said, grinning.

"You forgot to mention he's got the prettiest gals in the whole of Texas workin' here," a buxom raven-haired woman, who wore a low cut red silk gown, added. "Welcome home, Will."

"Georgia, you get back to peddlin' drinks to the customers," Simon ordered.

"Howdy, Jonas. Sorry about that little interruption. Glad to see someone's gonna ride herd on ol' Will."

"Howdy," Jonas answered. "It's more like the other way around. Will's gonna be ridin' herd on me."

"Then you're both in trouble. Pour yourselves a drink, fellers. The first one's on the house."

"Why thanks, Gordon," Will said. "Jonas, you're seein' history bein' made tonight. This old skinflint never buys anyone a drink."

"G'wan with you, Will." Simon snapped a bar towel at Will's chest. "I see another customer signalin'. We'll palaver a bit later."

"Sure enough," Will answered. He picked up the bottle, filled both glasses, and handed one to Jonas.

"To Kirkpatrick," he said. "May we survive the visit, and get the hell out of this town as fast as we can."

He touched his glass to Jonas's, downed the contents in one gulp, and poured himself another drink.

An hour later, the bottle was nearly emptied. Georgia had joined Will and Jonas at the table

164

where they'd moved. She commiserated with Will while he rehashed, yet again, his family turning against him when he joined the Rangers.

"Will, honey," she said. "I know Susan's the only one who realized why you *had* to get out of this town, and out of your ma and pa's grasps. But you've done everythin' you can to try and mend fences. It's up to your kinfolk to decide whether or not to realize you have the right to live the way you choose, and accept it. But you know you've always been able to turn to your sweet Georgia peach for comfort whenever you're feelin' low. Why don't we go up to my room and I'll cheer you up? It's always worked before."

"Uh-uh." Will shook his head. "Not tonight. I'm purely tempted, but me'n Jonas had better get on home."

"Are you certain?" Georgia ran a hand over his chest, then kissed him on the cheek.

Two cowboys were standing at the bar, working on whiskeys. One of them came over to the table and glared at Will.

"Kirkpatrick, you get away from Georgia," he warned, scowling. "You might think you've got a claim on her, but you lost that the day you left town. She's *my* gal, now."

"We were just talkin', is all, Taggart," Will said.

"It sure looked like more'n just talk to me. You want a woman, get that red-haired Irish gal your pa keeps around."

"He can't," Taggart's partner said, with a wicked chuckle. "His pa keeps that little red-headed spitfire all for himself. Mebbe he could settle for the colored woman. His brothers probably have."

Will clenched his fists and jumped up. He started for the two men. Jonas put a restraining hand on his shoulder.

"Don't, Will," he urged. "They ain't worth it. Think of your sister. You don't want to ruin her weddin' day by bein' in jail." He pushed Will back into his chair.

"Eli Taggart, I ain't your gal. Nobody else's, neither," Georgia said, after Will started to get back up, only to be shoved back down by Jonas again. "No man has a claim on me. That goes for you and your pal Jeb over there, too. You hear me, Jeb Bryant?"

"I figure different." Bryant downed the last of his glass and came over to stand next to Taggart. "Eli's spent enough buyin' you pretty little gee-gaws he's got the right to say you're his gal, even though you sure don't act like it most times."

"Well, you're both wrong," Georgia snapped. "Will, honey, like your friend says, these two ain't worth it. Just promise you'll stop by before you leave town."

"I wouldn't think of leavin' without sayin' goodbye," Will answered. "I reckon it's high time we called it a night. But I ain't done yet with you two boys. No one can say things like that about my father and get away with it. C'mon, Jonas."

When Will stood up, Taggart drove a hard right fist into his back, directly over his left kidney. Will arched with the pain, and fell to the sawdust covered floor, twisting to land on his back. Taggart drove at him, but Will recovered in time to drive both of his boots into Taggart's belly. The impact doubled him over, and sent him staggering back. Will scrambled to his feet and landed a left to the point of Taggart's chin. Bryant grabbed Will by the shoulder, spun him around, and smashed a fist into his jaw.

"Hey, two against one ain't fair," Jonas said, and jumped into the fray. He shot a quick left to the back of Bryant's neck, sending him stumbling forward. He hauled up against a post, then turned to face Jonas, who sent two quick blows into Bryant's gut. Bryant jackknifed, then slammed his head into the pit of Jonas's stomach, wrapped his arms around Jonas's waist, and smashed him into the wall.

The other patrons in the saloon stayed out of the fight, instead preferring to urge the combatants on, yelling for one side or the other to prevail, some placing bets on the outcome. The four men were trading blows back and forth, now.

Will had blood running from a cut under his left eye, and a lump rising on the right side of his jaw. Jonas's right eye was swollen and closed from a punch which Bryant had landed, and blood flowed freely from his nose. However, gradually, they were getting the better of their opponents. Will had flattened Taggart's nose with a vicious right, staggering him back, howling with the pain.

Jonas had discovered Bryant's belly was his weak point, so he kept punching at his middle, using a fierce combination of lefts and rights to keep battering Bryant's gut, until he could no longer drag air into his tortured lungs.

Bryant sagged against the wall, slid down it, and slumped onto his side. At the same time, Will ducked a punch from Taggart, sent one of his own wrist-deep into Taggart's belly, then when he folded, slammed a knee to his chin. Taggart dropped and lay still. Will and Jonas stood with their backs to the bar, chests heaving.

"I . . . I reckon we won," Jonas gasped.

"I would say so," Will answered. "Thanks for backin' me."

"Hey, that's what pards are for. Besides, they were playin' dirty. Taggart hit you in the back when you weren't lookin'."

"Could have been worse. He could've put a bullet in my back. I made a dumb mistake turnin' my back on him. There's your first big lesson as a Ranger, kid. Never turn your back on a man who's on the prod."

Before Jonas could answer, Marshal Spurr burst through the batwings. He carried a double barreled Remington shotgun, which he held level at his hip. Both triggers were already cocked.

"What the hell's goin' on in here?" he shouted.

"Not much anymore, Marshal," Simon answered. "Will and his pard pretty much settled things."

Spurr glanced at the two unconscious men on the floor, then at Will and Jonas.

"I should've known you'd be involved, Will," he said. "Gordon, someone better get Doc Wilson."

"I'll fetch him," one of the bystanders said.

"Thanks, Tommy," Spurr answered.

"I didn't start the fight," Will answered. "In fact, I tried to walk away from it."

"Will's tellin' the truth, Marshal," Georgia added. "Me'n him were just talkin' when Eli came over to bother us. He tried to claim I was his gal, no one else's. You of all men should know I don't belong to any one man, Marshal."

She winked, and Spurr blushed.

"Will and his friend were fixin' to go home anyway," Georgia continued. "When Will got up, Eli sucker punched him in the back. Will had no choice but to fight back. When he did, Jeb jumped into the fight, so Jonas had to help Will."

"Will and Jonas didn't want any part of this fight," Simon agreed. "Eli and Jeb forced it."

"Will, it seems you and your pard are off the hook," Spurr said. "You gonna want to press charges against these two yahoos?"

"No," Will said. "I just wanna get back to the house. I figure they've learned their lesson tonight, anyway. Long as it's all the same to you, me'n Jonas'll just mosey on home."

"Not quite so fast. I want the doc to check over the two of you before you leave."

"I don't need to see the doc, Max. Do you, Jonas?"

"Nope."

"It don't matter none what either of you *want,* you ain't leavin' this saloon until Doc Wilson checks you out," Spurr insisted. "Will, you're shaky on your feet, and Jonas, you're lookin' pretty wobbly too."

"That's just the red-eye we drank," Will protested. "We'll both be just fine."

"We'll let the doc decide that," Spurr answered. "Although, I will admit you both appear to be in far better shape than the other two."

Taggart had regained consciousness for just a moment, but only managed to roll onto his back before again passing out. Bryant was now semi-conscious, groaning, his arms wrapped around his middle. Spurr looked out the door.

"What the devil is takin' Doc Wilson so long?"

"He might've been out of his office, tendin' to someone," Simon said. "Don't worry. Tommy'll find him."

Spurr knelt alongside Taggart to ascertain if he was still breathing.

"Well, he'd better hurry. This one's still alive, but I'm not certain for how long. George, bring me a towel."

The bartender hurried over with one. Spurr took it and began dabbing the blood still dripping from Taggart's broken nose. He was about to ask Simon for another towel when Tommy returned, followed by the town physician, Dr. Toller Wilson.

Wilson was a young man, who was originally from back East, but had moved his family to Texas for the fresh air, milder climate, and to establish his own practice. He was slightly balding, so wore his dark hair very close cropped. Brown eyes peered out from behind a pair of pince-nez spectacles. While he was usually smiling, at the moment, taking in the scene in front of him, he wore a sober expression.

"Sorry it took me a few minutes," he said. "I was just finishing stitching up a bad gash in Harmon Malloy's leg when Tommy came for me. How many patients do I have, and which is in the worst shape?"

"Four," Spurr answered, from where he still knelt alongside Taggart. "This one right here

171

seems to be in the worst shape. He's havin' trouble breathin'."

Wilson hurried over to the downed cowboy and knelt by Taggart's side. He opened his medical bag, then began a quick examination.

"How bad is he, Doc?" Spurr asked, after Wilson had palpated Taggart's ribs, then listened to his heart and lungs through his stethoscope.

"He's in pretty bad shape, Marshal, but he'll live, unless there's internal injuries that I can't find, without a more thorough examination. He's havin' trouble breathing because his nose is busted, plus he's got a broken jaw. The jaw will have to be set, and he won't be eating anything besides beef broth or thin soup for quite some time. The abrasions and contusions—"

"The what?"

"Cuts and bruises, Marshal. They're nothing serious, but will need cleaning, dressing, and bandages. I'll need two men to carry him to my office. Place him on the examination table. I'll be right along."

"Don, Micah, pick him up and haul him to the doc's," Spurr ordered.

The two men Spurr indicated picked up Taggart to bring him to Wilson's office. The physician moved on to check over Jeb Bryant, who was now fully conscious, but still lying where he'd fallen, groaning. When Wilson pressed on his side, he yelled with pain.

"Doc, it feels like you just stuck a knife in my ribs! How bad is it?"

"You've taken a pretty good beating, that's for certain," Wilson answered. "You've got at least a couple of cracked ribs. I don't see any froth comin' from your mouth, and your breathing seems all right, so I don't believe any of them splintered and punctured a lung. You'll need to have a compression bandage wrapped around 'em to make certain that doesn't happen. You've also got a lot of other injuries that need to be treated. Do you have any tingling in your legs, or do they feel numb?"

"Uh-uh." Bryant shook his head.

"You think if someone helps you, that you'll be able to walk to my office?"

"I'll manage, Doc. Then, once I'm patched up, me'n Eli are comin' after Will and his pal."

"Neither one of you'll be doin' anything, except lying in bed for quite some time," Wilson answered. "Your friend's in far worse shape than you are."

"Try to use what little brains the Good Lord gave you, Jeb," Spurr said. "Everyone here says you and Eli started the fight. You're both damn lucky Will didn't want to press any charges, or you'd be goin' straight from the doc's to the jailhouse. Tony, get him outta here. Haul his sorry butt down to Doc Wilson's."

"Sure thing, Marshal."

Tony slid his arms under Jeb and helped him stand up, then draped Jeb's right arm over his shoulders.

"C'mon, Jeb. Let's get movin'. I've gotta be home before my wife starts wonderin' what happened to me. She's a worrier."

He half-carried, half-shoved the cowboy through the door.

"Will, good to see you again," Wilson said. "I can always count on business picking up whenever you ride into town. Let me take a quick look at you and your friend, then I'll have to get back home and start to operate on Eli Taggart's jaw. It's pretty badly shattered."

"Takin' a knee to the chin will do that, Doc," someone called out, with a laugh.

"Indeed," Wilson said. "Let me get back to work here."

He looked over Will's face, and turned his neck gently from side to side.

"I don't see anything major, Will. Let me just check your belly."

"You might want to check his back, too, Doc," Jonas said. "He took a pretty wicked punch to his lower back."

"Thanks, son," Wilson said. "Will, you'd better remove your shirt."

"Right here?" Will said. "In front of all these folks . . . and the ladies?"

"It's not like any of us gals haven't seen you

174

without your shirt on before, Will, honey," Georgia called out. Her eyes took on a devilish glint when she added, "Or the rest of your clothes, either. Doc, if he won't take off his shirt, I'll be happy to help you with that."

Will blushed as bright red as the letters on the sign over the door out front. Everyone else laughed.

"You're not helping, Georgia," Wilson said. "Although, if you don't remove that shirt, Will, I just might take her up on her offer."

"All right, you win," Will grumbled. Reluctantly, he shrugged out of his shirt. Wilson whistled when he saw the bruises covering Will's belly, and especially the one low on his back, where Taggart had sucker punched him.

"Will, I don't like the looks of some of those, particularly the one on your back," he said. "I hope your kidney hasn't been damaged."

He pushed on the bruise. Will winced.

"I don't know . . . I don't like the way you reacted."

"It's just a bad bruise, Doc. I've had far worse," Will objected. "If you're done, take a look at Jonas so we can get goin'."

"I want to clean out the cuts on your face," Wilson said. "Come with me to the office so I can do that. Then, I'll double-check your kidney and belly once I'm done with the other two men."

"If it's all right with you, it'd be just as easy for

me to let Delia do that at home," Will answered. "She's patched me up more'n once. She's as good at that as most doctors. No offense."

"None taken," Wilson answered. He rubbed a hand over his head. "It's against my better judgment, but I'll let you do that. However, if you become dizzy or nauseous, or when you pee if there's blood in your urine, or excessive pain, you get down to my office, right away."

"Will do, Doc. Can I put my shirt back on now?"

"Go ahead. I'll check your friend while you get yourself back together."

He turned his attention to Jonas.

"What's your name, son?"

"Jonas Peterson."

"How old are you?"

"A little more'n eighteen. I just signed on with the Rangers. They gave me Will as a pardner."

"Humph. Another young man who'll be havin' bullets dug out of him, and'll probably die from a gunshot way too young," Wilson said. "Well, let me take a look at you. Unbutton your shirt so I can make certain you don't have any deep bruises or other indications you may have suffered internal abdominal injuries."

Jonas complied, although albeit grudgingly. Wilson first examined the cuts and bruises on his face, then pushed against his stomach, along with light taps with the side of his fist, to see how

176

Jonas reacted. Jonas winced with each touch, but gave no sign of any sharp pain that would suggest torn muscles or ruptured organs, or any internal bleeding.

"You're in better shape than Will, but not by much," Wilson said. "I suppose I'd be wasting my breath to try'n talk you into coming down to my office so I can check you out more thoroughly, once I care for the more seriously injured men." He gave Will a meaningful look. "That would include you, Will."

"If Will ain't goin' to your office, then I ain't," Jonas said.

"And I already told you I don't need you to patch me up, Doc, even though I'm obliged for the offer," Will added.

"Suit yourselves," Wilson said, with a shrug. "I can't force either of you to allow me to treat you. But if one of you starts to feelin' sick to your stomach, light-headed, or begins spitting up blood, send for me—and I mean immediately."

"We'll do that, Doc," Will assured him. "How much do we owe you?"

"I'll put it on your family's account, as always," Wilson answered.

"Since it's for me, my father might not pay you," Will answered. "We haven't exactly been on good terms since I left home."

"You let me worry about that. I can handle your father," Wilson said.

"If you say so, Doc. Can we go now?"

"There's nothing more I can do, since neither of you will cooperate. You may as well head on home."

"Thanks, Doc. Will we see you at Susan's wedding?"

"Unless a medical emergency comes up that can't wait, yes."

"Good. We'll see you, then. C'mon, Jonas, button up your shirt and let's get outta here."

Will picked up his hat from where it had fallen and punched its crushed crown back into shape. Once Jonas had re-buttoned his shirt and retrieved his own hat, they made their good nights, and went out to their horses.

"It's gonna be another slow ride, Jonas," Will said, as he climbed painfully into his saddle, "but at least we don't have far to go. C'mon, Pete, let's get on home."

He and Jonas backed the horses away from the rail, and put them into a slow walk. Will just hoped they could get in the back door of the house without waking anyone but Delia.

Will and Jonas removed their boots and spurs on the back steps, then carried them into the house.

"Delia has a room off the kitchen," Will whispered to Jonas. "With any luck, she'll hear us come in, or else I can wake her without disturbin' the rest of the family. I don't feel like explainin' this to them right now. I want some sleep first."

A turned-low lamp was always left on in the kitchen. Will turned up the flame. He then knocked gently on Delia's door.

"Delia?" he whispered. When there was no response, he called again, a bit more loudly.

"Delia? It's Will."

"Master William? Hold on just a minute, child. I'll be right out."

She was used to being awakened at all hours of the night for emergencies. In fact, besides being a cook, she was a trained midwife, and had helped deliver all of the Kirkpatrick children.

There was a squeaking of bed springs, followed by a rustle of cloth as Delia pulled on a robe and slippers, then soft footsteps as she padded across the floor. Her eyes widened when she opened the door, and saw Will's cut and bruised face.

"Master William? What happened? You look like all the legions of Beelzebub attacked you!"

"Shh. I don't want to wake up the family. Me'n Jonas need your help, Delia."

"Master Jonas?" Delia took one look at him and gasped. "The both of you?"

"I'm afraid so, Delia," Will said. "We need you to fix us up."

"I'll do that, but you'll never be able to hide this from the rest of the family," Delia warned. "Not as bad as the two of you look."

"I know that, Delia, but I'd rather they not find out until morning."

"It already *is* morning," Jonas pointed out.

"All right, *later* this morning," Will answered.

"Enough." Delia took charge. "The two of you sit right down while I start some water boilin', then fetch some clean cloths and my medicines."

Delia went to work with the efficiency of a woman experienced in treating plantation injuries, gunshots, and other wounds common on the western frontier. Within a few minutes, she had the water hot, her supplies ready, and was cleaning out Will's and Jonas's wounds.

"Now, Master William, you tell me what happened to you boys."

"We were down at the saloon," Will said. "We'd had a few drinks, and were just gettin' ready to leave when two cowboys from the Double Diamond picked a fight with us. We tried to walk away, but they wouldn't let us."

"I've always warned you drinking whiskey was the devil's curse," Delia said. She shook her head in disgust.

"It wasn't the red-eye which started the fight, Delia," Jonas said. "Those two men said some terrible things, which made Will awful riled. I stopped him from goin' after 'em, and figured things would simmer down, but when we started to leave, one of 'em sucker punched Will in the back when he wasn't lookin'."

"That don't matter," Delia answered. "There's no words so terrible a body can't just walk away. You know, sticks and stones . . ."

"Delia, those two were sayin' things so crude I couldn't just sit there and take it," Will said. "Vulgar things about my father . . . and you and Peggy. Even so, Jonas stopped me, until Eli Taggart threw that first punch."

"Eli Taggart?" Delia grimaced. "I've crossed paths with him before. I'll bet Jeb Bryant was with him."

"He was," Will confirmed.

"In that case, I'll make an exception to what I just said. Those two men have the devil in their souls. They deserved whatever they got. I hope you gave them a good thrashing."

"We did." Will attempted to grin, but only managed to wince. "They'll be laid up at Doc Wilson's for quite some time."

"Perhaps while they're at the doctor's he could cut off their filthy tongues . . . and their—"

"Delia! I've never heard you talk like that."

"I'm sorry, Master William. However, those two men have been a scourge on this town ever since they arrived. If they're about, a woman can't even walk down the street without bein' subjected to their filthy mouths and foul language. I'll ask the Lord for His forgiveness after I finish tending to you boys. Now, hold still."

Delia washed out the cuts on Will's and Jonas's

faces, then uncorked a brown bottle. She poured a pea green, vile smelling liquid from it onto a clean cloth.

"What the he—I'm sorry, Delia, what the blue blazes is that stuff?" Jonas asked. "It smells awful."

"It might smell awful, but it'll heal your cuts faster than anythin' Doctor Wilson might put on them," Delia answered. "It's a mix of herbs, roots, and greens, which has been passed down in my family for generations."

"Listen to her, Jonas," Will said. "She's right. The stuff does smell awful, and it'll burn like— um, *heck,* but it'll keep any of these cuts from gettin' infected, and will heal 'em right quick."

"If you say so," Jonas answered, dubiously. "But I dunno."

"You'll see."

Delia coated Will's injuries with the liquid first, then covered the larger cuts with bandages. When she approached Jonas, he wrinkled his nose at the medicine's putrid odor.

"I'm thinkin' mebbe gettin' shot couldn't be worse than bein' treated with this stuff."

"You'd better hope you never find out," Will said. "Besides, you must've forgotten a Ranger has to handle everythin' thrown at him."

"I'd like to take some of this stuff to Cap'n Hunter and see what he says about that," Jonas retorted.

"Just hush, the two of you, so I can get this finished and we can all get some sleep," Delia ordered. She took another clean cloth, poured a good amount of the medicine onto it, and slathered it over Jonas's jaw. He had to bite his lips to keep from screaming at the burning pain. A few minutes later, the pain had subsided to a pleasant warmth, which seemed to suffuse his entire face. In a short while, Delia had treated all of his cuts. As she had done with Will, she covered the larger ones with bandages.

"There, now that wasn't so bad, was it, Master Jonas?"

"Except for the smell and pain, not at all," Jonas answered. "Thank you, Delia."

"It was no trouble . . . except for being woken up in the middle of the night, then tomorrow havin' to explain to Mr. and Mrs. Kirkpatrick why I didn't tell them what had happened, immediately. Now, the two of you get to bed. Rest is the best thing for you right now."

"Can't we help you clean up first?" Will asked.

"Have you forgotten I never allow anyone underfoot in my kitchen, Master William? Not even your mother or sister, let alone two stumble-footed boys. I'll straighten up by myself."

"Neither one of us is still a boy," Will protested.

"You'll always be one of my boys, and now, so will Master Jonas," Delia said. "So if you don't want me to take a switch to the two of you, get yourselves upstairs to bed, right now."

"Yes, *ma'am,*" Will said. "C'mon Jonas, I've been swatted enough for one night."

He and Jonas picked up their boots, then headed up to Will's room. Without even pulling back the covers or bothering to undress, they sprawled across the bed. Within ten minutes, they were both sound asleep.

10

Breakfast was always at 7:00 A.M. sharp in the Kirkpatrick household. Even though Will had told his father the previous night he and Jonas planned to sleep in, Delia still awakened them well ahead of time, but Will and Jonas were still ten minutes late to the table.

"We've been holding our meal for you two. Where the devil have you—" Will's father stopped short when he looked up, and saw their bruised and bandaged faces.

"What the hell happened to you?" he yelled, frowning. "Excuse my language, Claudette, Susan. You also, Peggy." The last was almost an afterthought. "I should have known something like this would occur, William. You're not even back home for a full day and you start trouble. I want an explanation, now, and it had better be good."

"Me'n Jonas . . . Jonas and I both want to apologize," Will answered. "However, we didn't start any trouble, and I'm not going to get into a long explanation about what happened. We were at the saloon when two cowboys started in hoorawin' us. We tried to avoid a fight, especially Jonas, but we couldn't."

"Will's right, Mr. Kirkpatrick. We tried to walk

185

away, but one of 'em sneak punched Will in the back, when he wasn't lookin'."

"That doesn't matter," Silas answered. "First of all, neither of you should have been in the saloon. Second, what could those men possibly have done to anger you enough to take part in fisticuffs?"

"In case you've already forgotten, Father, I told you *we* didn't want, nor start, the fight. The only reason it got as far as it did is we were defending this family's honor."

"What do you mean, William?"

"I'd rather not say in front of Mother, Susan, and Peggy."

"Claudette?"

"I believe I'd like to hear you answer your father's question, William."

"Well?" Silas's gaze bored into his oldest child.

"If you must know, they were saying vulgar, coarse things about you, Father. Absolute falsehoods about you and Peggy. Then they added more about Bertram, Gerard, and Delia."

"No!" Claudette swooned. Peggy hurried over to fan her. Susan looked properly shocked. Will's father and brothers stared at him in disbelief.

"You mean—" Silas said.

"You know exactly what I mean, Father. You asked for an explanation, and there you have it. Do you want to hear more? All the sordid details?"

"No. You've said more than enough."

Claudette had recovered sufficiently to also reply.

"I know I certainly do not want to hear any more! To think men would actually speak such horrible things in public. Especially when they aren't true."

"Remember, you're not in New Orleans any longer, Mother, nor back East. Manners are rougher out here. Not that 'proper' folks, no matter where they might live, don't love to gossip, also. I've heard some things that would shock any cowboy coming from the mouths of rich society ladies, when I've had to arrest their husbands."

"That is enough of this conversation," Silas said. "Peggy, you may start serving. After the Grace, I do have something to say to you and your friend, William."

"That's fine, Father."

Silas said a short prayer, then the family and Jonas began their meal.

"What I want to say to you, William, goes hand-in-hand with what I said last night. Neither you nor Mr. Peterson own the proper clothes to attend your sister's wedding. Therefore, I am going to stop at the haberdashery on my way to the bank, and tell Joseph you will be coming in for a fitting. I'm paying for the clothes. Don't even think of arguing," he said, when William started to object. "Either you allow Joseph to arrange proper dress for a wedding, or you won't be allowed to attend. Susan, you don't have a say in this."

"I suppose we can do that, since it's just one day, and it's for Susan," Will said. "We're going into town for haircuts, shaves, and baths anyway, so we'll stop at Joseph's after that."

"And no side trips to the saloon."

"Not a chance, Father. Last night was enough."

"Then we understand each other. As soon as breakfast is finished, we can all be on our way."

Twenty minutes before the shops and stores opened, Will and Jonas rode into town.

"There's Shalem's place, right there. Looks like he opened early," Will said. He pointed to a black-and-white sandwich sign that read: "Barbery Coast Tonsorial Parlor. Haircuts, Shaves, and Baths," in front of an otherwise unremarkable building. "He lived in San Francisco for a spell, so the name of his shop is a play on the Barbary Coast. Let's hope we're early enough to beat most of the other customers. Shalem's usually really busy."

They found a spot for their horses at the hitch-rail in front of the next building, left them there, and went inside the shop. One of the barbers was just pulling the cloth off a customer.

"Howdy, Shalem," Will said. " 'Mornin', Hugh."

"Will, good mornin'," Shalem Bencivenga, the first barber, answered. "I'd heard you were comin' back for the weddin'. Looks like you got here just in time. Another few days and no one'd be able to tell you from a bull buffalo. I assume your friend needs some sprucin' up, too."

"Yeah, we could both use some," Will said. "Good to see you again, Shalem. This here's my new pardner, Jonas Peterson."

"I've got a new partner, too. That's Jed Calhoun over there. Business has been so good, I had to put on another barber."

Bencivenga was a tall, slim man, in his mid- to late thirties. He wore his dark hair cut short, and had a full, neatly trimmed beard. Calhoun was much younger, probably around eighteen, certainly no more than twenty. He was a bit shorter than average, and still had the lankiness of youth. His blond hair was kept in an unusual style. It was shaved on the left side of his head, almost as if an Indian had started to scalp him but was interrupted, then kept long on top and combed over to the right, where it reached past his ear and almost to his shoulder.

"Howdy," Jed said. Will and Jonas returned his greeting.

"You boys take seats, and we'll be right with you," Bencivenga said. "I'm just finishin' up Hugh, here, then you'll be next. Good thing you got here when you did. We're gonna be extra busy today, with men gettin' ready for your sister's wedding tomorrow. Your pa and brothers'll be in after the bank closes."

Bencivenga brushed off Hugh Donnelly's shoulders.

"You're all set, Hugh" he said. "That'll be two bits."

Donnelly got up, gave the barber a quarter, then took his hat off a peg and put it on.

"Nice to see you again, Will, and to meet you, Jonas. Me'n Lorraine'll see you at Susan's weddin' tomorrow."

"We'll see you there," Will answered.

"Will, why don't you let me take care of you, and I'll have Jed take care of Jonas?" Bencivenga asked. "He's every bit as good a barber as I am."

"That's fine with me, as long as Jonas doesn't object," Will agreed.

"I'm so desperate to get this bramble patch on my head shorn, I'd even let a sheep shearer take scissors to me," Jonas answered.

"Great. Get in the chairs and we'll get to work," Bencivenga ordered. "Will, I assume you want the full treatment?" Bencivenga adjusted the chair once Will was seated. "Haircut, shave, hot and cold towels, bay rum, the knots rubbed out of your neck, shoulders, and face?"

"All of that, plus a hot bath," Will answered.

"I'd also like my hair cut pretty short. I'll be leaving as soon as Susan's wedding is over, and not certain when I'll be able to get my next haircut."

"How about you, Jonas?" Calhoun asked.

"The same as Will," Jonas answered.

"All right," Bencivenga said. "You're both in luck. Not only hasn't anyone made an appointment for a bath until later today, since you were here last, Will, I also added two more bathing rooms. I moved the second tub into one of them, and got a new one for the third. That means you'll have privacy while you take your baths, instead of havin' to share the same room. It also means even if someone comes in for a bath while you two are gettin' your haircuts and shaves, you won't have to wait for them to finish. It's a lot more pleasant for my customers, and brings in more money for me."

"I'm glad to hear you're doin' so well, Shalem," Will said. "How's the wife and kids?"

"They're doin' just fine. The kids are growin' like weeds. You'll see them tomorrow at your sister's wedding." He picked up a pair of scissors to begin cutting Will's hair. He and Will kept up a steady conversation while he worked, as did Jonas and Calhoun.

With both Will's and Jonas's hair and beards having grown so long, it was nearly an hour before they were finished. After holding up a

191

mirror so Will could see the back of his head, and approve the haircut, Bencivenga pulled the cloth off him.

"I always start heatin' water first thing in the mornin', so just give me and Jed a few minutes to fill the tubs, then you can take your baths."

"Those are sure gonna feel good," Will said, as he pulled himself out of the chair.

"You're both gonna smell a lot better, too," Calhoun added.

"Yeah, I have to admit, we both stink pretty bad," Jonas agreed.

Ten minutes later, Will and Jonas were settled in tubs filled with hot, soapy water. They lingered in their baths for more than an hour, letting the steaming liquid soak out the aches and grime of the trail. Finally, and reluctantly, they got out of the tubs, toweled off, and redressed.

"I was just comin' to check on you two," Bencivenga said, when they came back into the shop. "I was beginnin' to think you'd drowned."

"Nope. That water just felt so good I didn't want to leave," Will said.

"This is the cleanest I've been in so long I can't recollect the last time I felt this good," Jonas added.

"Glad to hear that," Bencivenga said.

"How much do we owe you, Shalem?" Will asked.

"Two bits for the haircuts, another two for the

192

shaves, and one for the baths, so three bits all together."

"That's just fine," Will said. He dug in his denims' right pocket, pulled out a silver dollar, and handed it to the barber.

"Keep the change,"

"Thanks, Will. Much obliged."

Jonas also gave Calhoun a silver dollar, plus a dime.

"Thanks for makin' me feel five pounds lighter, Jed."

"Glad to do it," Calhoun answered. "Yours was the toughest haircut and shave I've done since I started workin' for Shalem. I'm obliged to you for the practice."

"Where are you two headed now?" Bencivenga asked.

"We're on our way to Joseph's Haberdashery," Will told him. "Since we obviously don't have the right outfits for a wedding, my father stopped there this morning to make an appointment for us to get some."

"That sounds reasonable. Have a nice rest of the day, and we'll see you tomorrow."

"Thanks, Shalem. Nice meetin' you, Jed."

"The same goes for me," Jonas added. "*Adios*, for now."

"What the hell is a haberdashery?" Jonas asked Will, when they reined up in front of a shop which had "Mr. Joseph – Haberdasher. Fine Gentlemen's Clothing" lettered in gold leaf on both front pane glass windows.

"Beats the hell out of me," Will answered. "As far as I've been able to figure out, it's just a high-falutin' name for a store that sells only men's clothes, and not the kind I like to wear. My father and mother insisted all us boys buy our clothes here. I think the money he spends here is the only thing that keeps Joe Slattery in business. As soon as I was old enough to buy my own outfits, I got them at the general store instead. Well, let's get in there and get this over with."

Will patted Pete's neck after dismounting.

"Be glad I don't try'n dress you up like I've gotta be," he told the paint. "A fancy Indian blanket with fringes, and silver conchos and other shiny stuff all over your saddle. How'd you like that?"

In answer, Pete snorted, and shoved his muzzle against Will's chest, pushing him backward.

"You wouldn't, huh?" Will said, laughing. "Hell, neither would I. I'll be back quick as I can."

A young blonde woman behind the counter looked up when the two Rangers entered the store.

"William Kirkpatrick, as I live and breathe!" she exclaimed. "Father told me you and a friend would be in this morning, but I really didn't believe you'd show up, until I saw you with my own eyes. It's good to see you again."

"You too, Molly," Will answered. "This is my pard, Jonas Peterson. I've sure missed you, girl."

"Perhaps. But not enough to stay here in Kirkpatrick," she retorted.

"I suppose that's so," Will answered. "Although you are the only thing that might've made me stay."

Molly took a closer look at Will's bruised and bandaged face.

"I see being a Ranger has been good for you," she said, sarcastically.

"This? This is nothin'," Will said.

"Mr. Peterson, please forgive my rudeness," Molly said. "I'm still in a bit of shock from seeing William again. I'm very pleased to meet you. I'm Molly Slattery. My father owns this shop."

"Jonas. The pleasure is all mine, Miss Slattery. And a girl as pretty as you are could never be rude."

"Why, thank you, Jonas. See, Will, he knows how to flatter a lady. Perhaps he'll stay in town instead of you."

"I'm afraid not," Jonas said. "I'm a Ranger also. I'll be leaving with Will the day after his sister's wedding."

"More's the pity," Molly said. "I would have liked to get to know you better. Let me call father so he can get your clothes fitted. Will, your father has already picked them out. It's just a matter of making the alterations."

"That figures," Will muttered.

Molly disappeared into a back room, returning a moment later with her father, who, like her, had once been blond, but now was mostly bald, the little hair he did have faded to gray.

"Good morning, William," he said. "And you must be Jonas, from what Molly explained. Welcome to my shop."

" 'Mornin', Joseph," Will said. "Good to see you. How's your wife doing?"

"Joan's just fine," Slattery answered. "She'll be sorry she missed you, but of course you'll see her at the wedding. Now, shall I get both of your measurements so I'll have enough time to be certain the suits fit properly for the wedding? I have several others that also need to be tailored before the day is through."

"Might as well," Will said.

"Splendid." Slattery pulled two suits, shirts, pairs of socks, and ties from under the counter.

"William, you know where the fitting room is," he said. "Put yours on first, then once I mark them where the alterations are needed your friend can try his on. I just hope your father estimated your sizes correctly, so I don't have too much tailoring. This will be a rush order as it is."

"Sure thing," Will said. He picked up the

clothes and carried them into the fitting room in the back corner of the shop.

It took Slattery nearly an hour, fussing over every detail, before the suits and shirts were ready to be altered to his satisfaction. Both Will and Jonas had made his efforts even more difficult by insisting the shirt collars not be too tight. Finally, the garments were ready.

"You may come back for them any time after three," Slattery had told them. Now, they were standing in front of his shop, looking up and down Kirkpatrick's main street.

"Where do we go now, Will?" Jonas asked. "Back to your house?"

"No," Will answered. "First, we'll leave Pete and Rebel at the blacksmith's. They both need new shoes. Then, I've got to find a wedding gift for Susan and Harvey. After that, we'll head for the saloon. I dunno about you, but I can sure use a beer or two."

"I'm in your custody, per the judge's orders," Jonas answered, grinning. "I have to go where you go. What a pity it's such a hardship."

"I can see that it is," Will answered. "Let's go."

11

Saturday morning dawned exactly the way every bride hopes her wedding day will be. The sky was a clear blue, with just a few wispy mare's tail clouds, which only emphasized the cerulean vault of the heavens. The temperature was not too hot, only in the mid-seventies, and there was a slight northerly breeze which kept the humidity down.

Instead of using his own team of horses and carriage, or one from the Kirkpatrick Livery Stable for the bridal party, Silas Kirkpatrick had a team of matched white horses and a white carriage driven all the way up from Kerrville. The team and its driver had arrived the afternoon before, and the rig was now sitting in front of the Kirkpatrick mansion. The horses wore white plumes in their bridles, while the carriage was beribboned in white and gold.

Susan and her best friend and maid of honor, Sarah Thompson, were sitting in the rear, forward facing seat, while Juliet Mason, Ellen Hutton, and Emily Barton, the other bridesmaids, were sitting in the other. The rest of the Kirkpatricks, except for Will, were in the family's six passenger carriage, which had been polished by their driver, Jose Calderon, until its black leather paneled sides, red leather seats, and wood trim gleamed. The matched bays pulling the carriage also wore white plumes.

Will, despite his father's strenuous objections, had insisted on riding his own horse, so he was mounted on Pete, with Jonas next to him on Rebel, directly behind the carriage.

"It's time to go," Silas called out to Zeke Murray, the driver of Sarah's carriage. Murray nodded, slapped the reins on the rumps of his team, and put them into a high-stepping trot. It took only a few minutes before the small procession pulled up in front of the Kirkpatrick Community Christian Church. Most of the town, and the surrounding ranchers and their families, had been invited to the ceremony, and most of those who hadn't been, such as the owner of the saloon, the working girls from the establishment, ranch hands and others of the lower working classes, were standing on the boardwalk opposite the church, watching the bridal party and guests as they arrived.

Georgia, who was among their number, waved discreetly at Will, and gave him a sly wink. He touched two fingers to the brim of his Stetson in barely perceptible acknowledgement as he dismounted. He and Jonas tied their horses, then waited for the rest of Will's family to alight from their carriage.

Once the entire family, except for Susan and

her father, was inside the packed to overflowing church, Jacob, Henry, and Robert Prescott, Harvey's three younger brothers who were acting as ushers, escorted them to their pews. Harvey's mother and father had already been seated, while the groom and his best man, Adam Trumbull, whose family owned the neighboring Diamond T spread, were standing to the right of the altar.

When Silas had the church built, in the plans he included a small organ, which had been brought by rail as far as St. Louis, then freighted from there to the new town. When Susan and her father made their entrance, the organist began to play the *Bridal Chorus* from Richard Wagner's opera *Lohengrin*, which was more popularly known as *Here Comes the Bride.*

Once they reached the foot of the altar, Silas kissed Susan on the cheek, then took his seat alongside Claudette. Harvey, beaming with joy, took his place beside Susan, his soon-to-be bride. They made a handsome couple, she with her light brown hair and eyes and well-formed figure, he with his reddish-blond hair, blue eyes, and tall, slim build.

Reverend Frederick Schwarzwald, who had come from the German settlement of Fredericksburg some twelve miles to the northeast to take over the pastorship in Kirkpatrick, stood before the couple, opened his prayer book, and began the ceremony.

"Dearly beloved, we are gathered here today in the presence of Almighty God to join in holy matrimony Harvey Leroy Prescott and Susan Helena Kirkpatrick . . ."

The ceremony was brief. Less than thirty minutes after it began, Harvey and Susan Prescott walked out of the church to the strains of Felix Mendelssohn's *Wedding March*. They newlyweds emerged from the church to showers of rice thrown by friends and family, then climbed into their carriage to head for the reception at the Kirkpatrick home.

"Boy howdy, I'm sure glad that's over," Will said to Jonas, as he loosened his tie. "Not that I'm unhappy for Susan, but this damn tie's chokin' me."

"Yeah, but now the party's about to start," Jonas reminded him. "I'm sure lookin' forward to it. I ain't never been to a fancy affair in my entire life."

"That's true, but everythin' bein' the same, I'd just as soon head over to Gordon's saloon for some beers and his wife's baked ham, rather'n havin' to put on airs for my mother and father," Will said, as he untied Pete. "Reckon that's not an option, though."

He and Jonas climbed into their saddles, following the wedding party up the hill to the awaiting banquet.

• • •

The wedding reception for Susan and Harvey lasted well into the evening. Long tables laden with food had been set up in the Kirkpatrick's back yard, with Delia and Peggy efficiently running the buffet line and seating of guests.

A temporary dance floor had been laid, and two orchestras, one a seven member ensemble from Austin, the outer a five piece mariachi band from San Antonio, were providing the musical entertainment. Will had to wait his turn to finally get a dance with his sister, even having to wait until his younger brothers danced with her, despite protocol dictating he, as the oldest, should have had the first dance with her, after her new husband, and then their father.

"Will," she said softly as they waltzed, "thank you so much for coming home for my wedding. I really wasn't certain you would, after the huge argument you had with Mother and Father when you told them you weren't going into the bank, but had joined the Texas Rangers. I'm so proud of you, both for standing up to them and living the life you chose for yourself, and for what you're doing. I understand why you had to leave home and follow your own path. Now, if only you'd find the right woman to settle down with."

"Thanks, Susie," Will said. "You always were the only one who understood me. As far as coming home, I nearly didn't, but Captain Hunter and Father didn't leave me any choice. They were right. I wouldn't have missed being here for your special day for anythin'. As far as the woman, when the right one comes along, I'll know it."

"I'm so glad," Susan said. "Your wedding gift was lovely, also. How in the world did you find that lovely Navajo blanket, and have it embroidered with mine and Harvey's name and our wedding date, in time for today?"

"It wasn't easy," Will answered. "Luckily, Hank at the general store had just gotten a shipment in, and Ada Hopkins was able to do the embroidery. I'm glad you like it."

"Why wouldn't I? It's perfect. Harvey and I will be able to snuggle together under it on cold, windy nights. Perhaps we'll even—"

"I think you've said enough," Will said, grinning.

"Now you sound like Mother," Susan said. "Always saying a decent girl must be prim and proper, and know her place. Well, that's just not me. You know that, and Harvey knows it. Now that I'm out of this house, everyone else is about to know it, too. I'm sick and tired of being a good little girl."

"That means I'm probably the only one in the family who understands *you*," Will said.

"Which is why we've always gotten along so well, big brother. Don't forget to thank Jonas for me and Harvey again, for his present. He didn't really have to get us anything, since his invitation was spur of the moment. I know he doesn't have much money, but the china tea set was just perfect."

"You can tell him yourself," Will said. The music had stopped, and the dancers were applauding the orchestra. "I see him headed this way. I do believe he intends to ask you for the next dance."

"Ooh." Susan gave a soft squeal of delight. "Mother will be deliciously scandalized, and Father, well, if I hadn't gotten married, he'd have confined me to the house for a month, as punishment for dancing with a man I've just met. Perhaps I'll even kiss Jonas while we dance. That will really cause a stir. Remember two things, Will. I love you, and I always will. You'll always be welcome to stay with me and Harvey, if Mother and Father won't welcome you back. That, and keep yourself safe."

"Thanks, Susie. I'll do my best. You and Harve watch yourselves in New Orleans, too. I know it's a great place for a honeymoon, and Mother is from there, but there are also parts of the city you need to stay clear of."

Will kissed her on the cheek, just as Jonas stepped up to them.

"May I have the next dance, Mrs. Prescott, with your brother's kind permission, that is?" he asked.

"You certainly may, Mr. Peterson. And I don't need my brother's permission, nor anyone else's, to dance with whomever I choose."

The mariachi band took over, and broke into a lively border tune. Susan took Jonas in her arms and swirled him away.

"I sure hope Harve knows what he's let himself in for," Will murmured to himself. "He's about to start a wild ride."

12

Since the reception didn't end until well after midnight, Will and Jonas weren't up with the sun, as they usually would have been. In fact, they awoke so late they decided to stay one more day, and leave early Monday morning. They rode out of Kirkpatrick just before eight o'clock. Will's farewell to his family had been fraught with tension, his mother pleading with him one last time to give up the Rangers, come home, and go to work in the family's bank. Now, three hours and fifteen miles after leaving town, the two men had stopped alongside a small spring, to eat a quick meal of hardtack and jerky, and allow the horses a breather.

"Someone's comin' fast," Will said, at the hoof beats of a hard ridden horse coming to his ears. "Don't know if he means trouble or not, but we'd better be ready." He pulled out his six-gun, while Jonas loosened his in its holster. The hoof beats drew nearer, then Kirkpatrick's deputy marshal, Art Mason, rode into view. A bloody bandage was tied around his right arm. He slid his lathered sorrel to a crow-hopping halt. The horse stood blowing hard, head hung low and spraddle-legged.

"Art. What the hell happened to you?" Will asked.

"I'm sure . . . glad I caught up to . . . you fellers," Mason said, gasping for breath. "The Kirkpatrick bank's been robbed."

"What?" Will said.

"The bank's been robbed. Four or five men hit it just after the doors opened. Plugged Newt Haines, the head teller, and cleaned out the cash drawers. Mebbe the vault, too. I dunno. They shot their way outta town. That's when I caught this bullet. The marshal sent me to find you boys while he went after the bunch, but he won't be able to chase 'em too far, since he's got no jurisdiction outside of town."

"You can tell us the rest as we ride," Will said. He and Jonas tightened their cinches and jumped into their saddles.

"Let's go!"

The men put their horses into a gallop.

"Anybody else hurt, besides Newt?" Will asked.

"Not that I know of. I know your father and brothers weren't, except for a knock on the head Bertram took, when he didn't move fast enough to suit those *hombres*," Mason answered. "It's just lucky you fellers weren't ridin' all that hard. I figured I wouldn't catch up with you for at least another hour."

"How bad was Newt hit?"

"Pretty bad, from what I could see. Appeared like he was gut-shot. I don't imagine he's gonna pull through. Doc Wilson'll do all he can for him, though. He's a fine doctor."

"Anybody get a look at any of those outlaws, or what kind of horses they were ridin'?"

"They were all masked. The horses weren't any different from a hundred others, all bays or chestnuts."

"Any of 'em get winged?"

Mason shook his head. "Doesn't seem so. If one of 'em did, he wasn't hurt bad enough to slow him down any. Look, I'm slowin' you boys down. My horse is plumb wore out. You ride on ahead. You don't need me."

"What about your arm?" Will asked.

"It'll be all right. I lost a good chunk of flesh, and bled a lot, but Doc Wilson'll take care of it proper when I get back. Don't worry about me. Those *hombres'll* have a big enough start on you as it is, without me holdin' you back."

"All right. You take care, Art."

"And you two be careful. Hope you find those *hombres*."

"We will. You can count on it," Will said. "C'mon, Pete, move those feet."

He and Jonas urged their mounts to even greater speed.

When Will and Jonas reached Kirkpatrick, Marshal Spurr was sitting in front of his office, waiting for them. With him were Will's father and brothers, as well as several townspeople. Bert sported a clean white bandage wrapped around his scalp.

"Will. Jonas. Glad to see Art found you. Where's he at?" Spurr said.

"He had to stop and rest his horse," Will answered. "I don't suppose you caught up with the men who did this. How are you doin', Bert?"

"I've got one hell of a headache, but I'll be all right," Bertram answered.

"No, I sure didn't," Spurr said in answer to Will's first question. "I lost their trail about six miles north of town, so I came back here to wait for you fellers. I figure if I show you where the tracks petered out you might be able to pick 'em up again."

"You'll be ridin' with us," Will answered. "I'll deputize you, so you'll have full authority. Grab what supplies you need and be ready in ten minutes. I'll meet you back here."

"Where are you goin'?" Spurr asked.

"Doc Wilson's. If Newt Haines is still alive, I want to see if he can talk. Jonas, you stay here, and talk to my father and brothers. Get as much information from 'em as you can. Then we'll be ridin'."

Will backed Pete away from the office, and spurred him into a lope, until he reached the doctor's office, which was located in a wing of his house. He dismounted, hurried up the walk, and went inside.

"I'll be right with you," Doctor Wilson called from the back room.

"It's Will Kirkpatrick, Doc. I'm takin' after the trail of those bank robbers, soon as I see if Newt is in any shape to talk."

Wilson came out from the back, wiping his hands on a blood-stained towel.

"He's not, and I'm afraid he won't be, Will. He took a bullet in his abdomen, at close range. His intestines have been really torn up, I'm certain. It's just a matter of time. At the rate he seems to be hemorrhaging, I'd give him an hour or two at the most. Real shame. He was engaged to Mary Kline. They were supposed to be married this summer. I had to give her a sedative, then send her home."

"Thanks, Doc. I've gotta get on the trail of those renegades. The marshal will be ridin' with me and Jonas. If Newt does happen to regain consciousness, even for a few minutes, see if he can tell you anythin' at all about the robbery. Anythin' he can give you, no matter how small, might just help. When Art Mason gets back, if Newt is still alive, have him stay here until Newt dies, just in case he can talk with him."

"I'll do that," Wilson answered.

"Thanks, Doc. I'm obliged. *Adios*."

"*Vaya con Dios*, Will. And good luck. When

you do catch up to those men, if you have to shoot any of them, try'n keep them alive, so I can patch them up for the hanging."

"That's a promise, Doc."

Will retrieved his horse and went back to the marshal's office. Jonas and Spurr were already mounted and waiting for him. Spurr was on a sturdy sorrel gelding he'd named Durango.

"How's Newt?" Will's father asked.

"No good." Will shook his head. "It's just a matter of a few hours, at most. The slug he took tore up his guts real bad, Doc Wilson said."

"William, I'm asking you to forget our differences, at least for now," Silas said. "Just find and bring back the men who did this."

"I will, Father. Not just because it's my family's bank that was robbed, but because it's my job. You have my word on it, as your son, and a lawman. I do need one favor in return."

"Whatever it is, just ask."

"I need a telegram sent to Captain Hunter at Ranger Headquarters in Austin, explaining what happened, and tellin' him me'n Jonas are on the trail of those outlaws."

"I'll have that done right now."

"Thanks. We'll be back as quick as we can, with those men in tow . . . either alive, or draped belly-down over their saddles. Tell Mother not to worry. Oh, and I wouldn't send word to Susan about this, either. Let her'n Harve enjoy their honeymoon. No need to have 'em worryin' and frettin'. There's not a thing they can do anyway."

"That's good advice, Will," Gerard said. "I'll see that Father takes it."

"Good," Will answered. "We've wasted enough time palaverin'. Jonas, Max, let's ride."

Spurr pointed to where the hoof prints of five horses turned off the main road to Fredericksburg.

"Here's where they turned off the road, and started cross-country."

"Yep, the tracks are pretty plain," Will said.

"For about another mile," Spurr answered. "Then I lost 'em on some hardpan. I'm hopin' you'll be able to pick 'em up again, Will."

"We'll see," Will answered. He pushed Pete back into a lope. A bit more than a mile farther, the tracks disappeared on a stretch of gravel and rock.

"This is where I lost 'em," Spurr said.

"They seemed to be headed northeast. We'll ride a little way in that direction and see if we can pick 'em up again," Will answered.

At a slow walk, Will moved Pete forward. He leaned over in his saddle, scanning the ground from side to side, looking for any sign of the outlaws' passing.

"Seems to be some horse droppin's up ahead," Jonas pointed. "Let's hope that means we've picked up the trail again."

"You've got good eyes, Jonas," Will said.

They rode up to the mound of manure. Will dismounted and squatted on his haunches next to the pile. He picked up some of the droppings in his hand, sniffed at them, then crumbled them between his fingers.

"They're about six hours ahead of us," he said, as he wiped off his hand on his denims, then straightened up. "I was hopin' they hadn't kept pushin' that hard, but it could be worse. They'll have to slow up to give their horses a break before much longer. Let's go.

"There's somethin' hangin' off that bush up ahead," Will said, a few hundred yards later. He plucked the object from the shrub. "Yep, it's a hank of hair from a bay or black horse's tail. We're still on their trail. It'll be harder to keep on it, on this ground, but they ain't gonna give us the slip that easy."

Now, following the tracks of the bank robbers became a slow, painstaking process. Will had to scour the ground and vegetation for the slightest sign, a scrap of cloth snagged on an ocotillo wand's spines, a bit of horsehair caught in a cholla's needles, broken twigs where horses and men had passed, snapped off mesquite branches where a passing horse had decided to snatch a mouthful of leaves. Occasionally, on a stretch of soft or sandy ground, the outlaws' trail once again became clear.

Will pulled Pete to a stop as dusk fell.

"This is as far as we go for today," he said. "It's gettin' too dark to follow sign. We'll make camp here for the night, get some rest for both us and the horses, and start out fresh at first light."

"Are we gainin' any on 'em, Will?" Jonas asked.

Will shook his head.

"No. In fact, they've gained some on us. I expected that. They know where they're goin', so they can just keep on ridin', while we have to keep searchin' for sign. I ain't worried, though. Sooner or later, they'll start to relax and move slower, figurin' they've made a clean getaway. That's when we'll start catchin' up to 'em. And we *will* find 'em. I'll bet my hat on it."

"No offense, Will. But that old Stetson of yours ain't much of a hat," Spurr said. "You ain't riskin' a whole lot."

"There's nothin' wrong with my hat," Will retorted. "It's just broken in."

"Mebbe so, but it's pretty pathetic lookin'," Jonas said. "Kinda like it was shot, then stomped by a crazed bronc, then thrown in the river and stampeded into the mud by a herd of maddened cows."

"Enough about my hat. Let's get settled," Will ordered.

The horses were cared for first, as always, then Will built a small, almost smokeless fire.

After eating their bacon, beans, and biscuits, and downing several cups each of thick, black coffee, the men rolled in their blankets. Jonas and Spurr were soon asleep, while Will stared up at the stars sprinkled across the night sky.

Funny how things turn out sometimes, he thought. *I leave home to get away from my father, and now I'm chasin' the outlaws who robbed his bank. Whoever would've guessed? Well, if I am gonna catch up to those hombres, I'd better get some shut-eye.*

He rolled onto his belly, slid his Peacemaker out of its holster, put it where it would be within easy reach if needed, then pulled the blanket over his shoulders. Five minutes later, his soft snores joined those of his comrades.

Two-and-a-half days later, Will and his partners reined their horses to a stop on the banks of the Colorado River.

"It's just like I told you boys yesterday," Will said. "Those *hombres* are headin' for the Balcones canyons. I was afraid of that. It looks like they'll get there ahead of us. If they do, we'll sure have a helluva time rootin' 'em outta there."

The Balcones canyons, although not much more than forty miles from Austin, were as rugged a wilderness as any found in Texas. It was made up of a jumble of deep canyons, free-running streams, and rock terraces. Several of the streams formed waterfalls as they tumbled over the rocks and ledges. Heavily forested with oak, elm, hickory, sycamore, cottonwood, and even some big-toothed maple, the Balcones were an ideal spot for hunting and fishing . . . or a perfect hiding place for men on the run from the law.

"How far behind 'em do you think we are, Will?" Jonas asked.

"No more'n a couple of hours, now. But that's more'n enough time for those *hombres* to disappear into the canyons. There's no point puttin' this off. Let's get on in there."

The three men put their horses into the swirling blue waters of the Colorado. In mid-stream, the mounts had to swim for several hundred feet. They emerged from the river dripping wet, and shook themselves vigorously, much to the chagrin of their riders.

"Now that we're across, which way do we head, Will, upstream or down?" Spurr asked.

"The deeper canyons are still downstream, so we'll head that way. I've got a gut feelin' that's the way our men headed."

"My hunches have played out plenty of times," Spurr said. "I'm sure not gonna doubt yours."

They put the horses into motion once again. A quarter-mile later, Will's hunch proved accurate. He pointed to several hoof prints in the damp sand along the riverbank.

"There's the tracks we're lookin' for. Those

hombres sure aren't worried about anyone tryin' to follow 'em into the Balcones. They ain't even tryin' to hide their tracks. We'll make better time now. We should come up on 'em before sundown. C'mon."

He put Pete into a slow lope, which would cover plenty of ground, but still allow Will to follow the outlaws' trail with no trouble.

Two miles later, the outlaws' tracks turned away from the river, into a wide, deep, and heavily wooded canyon.

"We go slow and easy from here on in," Will warned. "This is an ideal spot for an ambush. Keep your eyes peeled and your ears open."

He turned Pete into the canyon, with Jonas and Spurr close on their heels. The trail wound along the left side of a good-sized stream which ran through the canyon. The canyon's left wall was not nearly as steep as its right, and was marked by shallows and wide, sandy banks along the stream. The right was much steeper, in places sheer rock walls, which rose nearly vertically from the canyon's floor.

Jonas looked up at the top of one of those cliffs and shook his head.

"Those *hombres* could pick us all off from up there before we even knew what hit us. You think they might've spotted us?"

"*Quien sabe?*" Will said. "If they're smart, they've got a man watchin' their back trail."

"Don't see how they could've gotten up there, anyway," Spurr said.

"That's right. So far, there hasn't been any place to cross," Will agreed. "We should be all right, unless they ducked into the trees and have doubled back on us. Just keep alert. Pay attention to your horses, too. They'll probably smell or hear somethin' long before we do."

Another half-a-mile into the canyon, the trail crossed the stream, then continued up a steep ridge on the other side.

"Here's where it could get real interestin'," Will muttered. "We'd better hope those *hombres* aren't on the other side, waitin' until we get midstream, where they can cut us down real easy. I'm not certain how deep the water is where it runs up against the other wall. Pull out your guns and hold 'em over your heads to make certain they stay dry."

After pulling out his own weapons, Will put Pete into the stream. The water came to just over belly deep on the horses when they reached the far side of the stream. Pete, in the lead, lunged from the water and up the bank. Rebel and Durango were right behind, snorting their displeasure.

"Well, we made it across without gettin' plugged, and we didn't get all that wet," Will said. "Let's keep on movin'. We're sittin' ducks right here, and if we don't come up with those renegades before dark, they're liable to give us the slip."

He slid his six-gun back into its holster, his rifle back into its scabbard, and heeled Pete into a walk once again.

The trail climbed steeply for several hundred yards, then leveled off, winding through the wooded terrain above the canyon's rim. The hoof prints of the outlaws' horses were still plain. There was still no sign of the lawmen's quarry, and their horses gave no indication of anyone nearby. Will and his partners had just rounded a bend when several rifle shots rang out in front of them. Spurr yelled out in pain.

"I've been hit!"

He'd no sooner done this than more shots rang out, this time from behind.

"Ambush! They've got us in a crossfire!" Will shouted. "Get into the woods and head back for the stream. Follow me!"

He whirled Pete and sent him crashing into the forest undergrowth. Bullets smacked into tree trunks as the outlaws attempted to gun down the fleeing lawmen.

"Keep movin' until we reach the water," Will ordered. "Max, how bad are you hit?"

"I don't think too bad," Spurr said. "Took one in the side, but I don't think the slug's still in me. Seems to be just a crease."

"Can you hold on until we reach a place to hole up?"

"I'll manage."

"Lemme know if you can't."

Will led his partners on a mad dash for safety, weaving in and out of the trees, pushing the horses through thickets and brambles. When they came out atop a steep drop that led down to the river, Will didn't hesitate. He dug his spurs deep into Pete's sides, sending the paint over the edge, into a scrambling, sliding drop to the stream below.

The water had undercut the stream bank at that point, so Pete hit the water hard. The impact drove him to his knees, and he half rolled, dumping Will into the water. Spluttering, Will scrambled to his feet, pulled out his Colt, and began a covering fire for Jonas and Spurr, whose horses were still plunging madly down the bank.

A red streak showed on the right side of Spurr's blue shirt. The marshal also wore a pair of yellow cavalryman's suspenders. One more shot rang out before Spurr reached the water, and the suspender over his right shoulder snapped when the bullet clipped it. Rebel dropped into the stream a moment before Durango. Both men jumped from their saddles, and began returning the outlaws' fire.

Will had emptied his revolver, so he yanked his Winchester from its scabbard and waited.

Three horses and riders appeared on the bank above, unaware of the danger waiting below, in their determination to kill their pursuers. Two were able to pull their horses to a sliding stop. The third could not jerk back on the reins in time to stop his chestnut from slipping over the brink. Halfway down, his horse stumbled, then toppled end over end, throwing his rider, who hit the rocky ground head first, snapping his neck. His body slid to within twenty feet of the stream, where it became tangled in a blackberry thicket.

Will aimed his rifle at the two men above and took two quick shots, the first one striking one of the men in the chest, knocking him backward out of his saddle. Will's second bullet tore into the remaining man's belly. The outlaw screamed, doubled over, and fell over his horse's neck, then slid to the ground. He rolled over the edge, down the slope, and tumbled into the river. His body floated face down for a hundred yards, until the current carried it close to shore and it snagged on a downed tree.

The last two outlaws, thinking the three soaking wet lawmen in the stream still made easy targets, jumped from their saddles and bellied down at the top of the embankment. One pushed himself up slightly to take aim at Will. When he did, Jonas and Spurr fired at the same time. Jonas's bullet missed, but Spurr's took him just below the throat, angling upward through his neck and exiting from the base of his skull.

The last man took careful aim and shot at Will. Luck was with the Ranger, for his foot slid off a rock on the slippery stream bed, dumping him back into the water. The bullet which had been intended for his chest whined harmlessly over him, and ricocheted off a boulder on the opposite bank. Jonas's return shot at the outlaw hit him just above the bridge of his nose, and buried itself in his brain.

"You think we got 'em all, Will?" Spurr asked, as silence descended on the canyon.

"I think so, but be careful, just in case one's playin' possum," Will answered. "Max, check the one that fell off his horse. Jonas, get the one who's hung up on that log. Get his horse, too."

The horse which had tumbled into the river had somehow escaped any injuries but a few cuts and scrapes, and was standing alongside Rebel, still clearly shaken after his ordeal.

"I'm goin' back up to get those other three men, and their horses. You two get to the other side of the stream. Take Pete with you. Soon as I'm back, I'll check your hurts, Max. And you might want to pull your pants back up. It's plumb embarrassin' seein' you like that. Georgia might be right pleased, though."

Between the bullet torn suspender, and the weight of his holster pulling on them, Spurr's soaked tan canvas pants had dropped over his right hip, exposing his underwear.

Jonas laughed. Spurr pulled his pants back up to his waist.

"That's better," Will said. "Once we're finished pickin' up those *hombres*, we'll camp here for the night. The sun'll be down in less'n an hour, so we wouldn't get far anyway. We'll stay here, dry out, let the horses rest, and start out at sunup."

"You gonna be able to make that climb, Will?" Jonas asked.

"I'll make it all right," Will assured him. "The only question is will I be able to convince those horses to follow me back down. While you're waitin' for me, you might want to get a fire started."

"Will do."

Jonas and Spurr went to retrieve the bodies in the river and in the blackberry bushes. Will had a tough time climbing the steep slope, but, using every handhold he could find, dropping to his belly and dragging himself along by pulling himself from bush to bush when necessary, he reached the top and pulled himself onto level ground about twenty minutes later. He checked the three dead men, then rounded up their horses. He lifted the bodies onto the horses' backs and lashed them in place, then climbed into the saddle of the one which seemed calmest, a flea-bitten gray gelding. He held tightly to the reins of the other two animals.

"You ain't gonna be too happy with me until this is over," he told the horses, "but there's plenty of grass waitin' on the other side, and you won't be pushed so hard after tonight. Let's go."

He picked up the gray's reins and clucked to him. When they reached the top of the slope, the gray hesitated, and the other two horses pulled back, snorting. Will spoke soothingly to them, then touched his spurs to the gray's sides. The horse whinnied nervously, and plunged over the bank, the other two horses pulled along by Will's firm grip on the reins. This descent was every bit as dangerous as the first, with Will having to control three frightened horses and their grisly burdens. Somehow, he made it safely down the slope, then crossed the river.

"Boy howdy, neither one of us thought you were gonna make it," Jonas said. "Seems like the Good Lord was watchin' over you."

"Somebody sure was, that's for certain," Will said. He dismounted, and Pete trotted up to him to nuzzle his face. Will patted his neck.

"I'll take care of you in a few minutes," he promised. "Soon as I check Max. Jonas, gimme a hand untyin' these men."

"I'll help with that, too. I ain't hurt all that bad," Max said. "The bleedin's already stopped, at least, just about."

225

"Better let me check you anyway," Will answered. "There's no sense in chancin' blood poisonin'."

"All right. Soon as we get these bodies off the horses."

"After we're done with that, I'll get some more wood for the fire while you're tendin' to Max, unless you need my help, Will," Jonas said.

"No, you go ahead and do that," Will answered. "Unless you think you're gonna pass out, Max."

"Me? Not a chance," Max said.

After the bodies of the three bank robbers Will had retrieved were taken off their horses and laid alongside their two companions, Will turned his attention to Spurr. He took a small, oilskin wrapped bundle from his saddlebag, unwrapped it, and took out a small leather bag. From that he removed a strip of bandage, small bottle of carbolic solution, and a tin of ointment, while Max removed his shirt and dropped the top half of his red woolen underwear to his waist.

"See, I told you it ain't all that much," he said to Will.

"It's not all that bad, but it is deep enough it needs some stitches," Will answered. "You've also got a bullet burn across the top of your shoulder. I'll just put some salve on that one. Lemme get my needle and thread. I'll get some whiskey for you, too."

Will pulled out a heavy needle and thick thread from the medical kit, and a flask of whiskey from his saddlebag. He gave Max a swallow of the liquor, then used more of it to wash out the wound in his side. Once that was done, he stitched the wound shut, poured carbolic over it, coated it with salve, wrapped a bandage around Spurr's middle and tied it in place.

"You can put your shirt back on now," he told Spurr, once he was finished.

"I reckon I'll just leave it off for awhile, and put it on the rocks near the fire to dry. I sure don't want to catch a chill, with night comin' on," Spurr answered.

"That's not a bad idea," Will said. "Reckon I'll do the same."

Will pulled off his shirt, picked his and Spurr's up, and spread them out on the side of a large rock alongside the fire. Jonas returned, carrying an armload of dried branches.

"Reckon I'd better dry my shirt, too," he said. He dropped the wood next to the fire, then peeled off his drenched shirt and spread it alongside the others. Max settled alongside the fire.

"If you're gonna be all right, Max, me'n Jonas are gonna search those bodies, and their saddlebags, to see if we can figure out who they were, and hopefully find the stolen money," Will said.

"I'll be fine. You go right ahead," Spurr

answered. "I reckon I'm gonna take off my boots and socks to dry them, too. I'll just rest and let you boys do all the work."

"Okay. C'mon, Jonas. We'll go through the saddlebags first."

Jonas followed Will to where the horses were grazing, at a good-sized patch of grass. They began going through the outlaws' saddlebags.

"I've got some cash in this one, Will," Jonas said.

"Same here," Will answered.

Their search revealed each outlaw had carried a thousand dollars.

"Hardly seems worth murderin' someone, then gettin' yourself killed, for that little money," Jonas said.

"You're right. If they cleaned out the bank vault, like Art said they did, they should've had more. I doubt they had time to cache the rest anywhere. Plus, we saw no sign they'd stopped on the way, nor any fresh dug ground, neither. Let's check the bodies. Mebbe we'll find somethin' there."

The five dead men's pockets were searched, but revealed nothing of interest, no clue to their identities. Will and Jonas studied their faces carefully.

"You recognize any of 'em, Will?" Jonas asked.

"No. The one you drilled through the face looks sorta familiar, but I can't be certain."

"I don't recognize any of 'em, either. What're we gonna do with 'em?"

"We're gonna wrap 'em up real tight, hope the weather stays kinda cool so they don't get to stinkin' too much, and haul 'em back to town," Will answered. "Mebbe somebody there will know who they are."

"Were." Jonas corrected.

"I guess you're right. Were," Will answered, with a grim laugh.

The bodies were wrapped in blankets, then the gear removed from the horses, who werc rubbed down and picketed to graze. After that was done, Will and Jonas returned to the fire, where Spurr had dozed off. They also took off their boots and socks to dry. Will made the usual trail supper of bacon, beans, biscuits, and coffee. Spurr awakened at the smell of the frying meat and boiling coffee. Once supper was finished, the horses were checked one final time, then the three worn-out lawmen turned in for the night.

13

Late in the afternoon three days later, Will and his partners rode into Kirkpatrick. By the time they reached the marshal's office, a good-sized crowd had gathered, and followed them. Deputy Art Mason had heard the commotion, and was waiting for them on the front sidewalk.

"Howdy," he said to them. "I see you've caught the rest of the gang."

"The rest of the gang?" Will echoed. "What do you mean, 'the *rest* of the gang'?"

"Newt Haines hung on long enough to talk before he died," Mason answered. "He told me the whole story. I've got the leader locked up. You'd better come inside, Will. You ain't gonna be happy."

"All right," Will said. "Have some men take these bodies down to the undertaker, will you? Make certain he leaves their faces uncovered, so we can see if anyone recognizes them."

"I'm already here," Frederick Eagle, the town undertaker, called out from the back of the crowd. "I'll take charge of them."

"Fine, Fred," Will answered. "Max, Jonas, I figure you'd better come along, too."

They dismounted and followed Mason inside

the office. Will stopped short when he saw the occupant of the first cell.

"Art! Is this some kind of bad joke?"

"I wish it was," Mason answered.

"William, it's about time you returned," his father called, from where he sat on the edge of the cell's bunk. "Perhaps now you can explain to this jackass that I had nothing to do with robbing my own bank, so I might be released from this imprisonment. Did you capture the real perpetrators?"

"We caught up with 'em, and had to shoot it out with the gang when they ambushed us," Will said. "They're all dead. We got back five thousand dollars. Each man had a thousand with him."

"But they took over fifty thousand," Silas answered. "Where's the rest? You need to get to the bottom of this, William."

"I intend to do exactly that," Will answered. "Art, what's the meaning of this? I know my father. He's a ruthless businessman, but he is honest. He'd never steal money from folks who entrusted it to him. Besides, what reason would he have? It's ridiculous locking him up."

"That's what I tried to tell him, William. It's preposterous to even imagine I would steal from my friends, the people who helped me build this town."

"Just simmer down, Mr. Kirkpatrick, and let me

talk to your son," Mason said. "Will, let's go out front, where we can speak in private."

"I'd like to hear your explanation too, Art," Spurr said. "I also find it impossible to believe that Silas would rob his own bank."

"He didn't," Mason answered. "But he sure planned and arranged it."

The men went back to the front office. Mason locked the door and pulled down the shades before he spoke.

"We might as well all sit down," he said. "This will take a while."

Once everyone was seated, he took a file from the top desk drawer and handed it to Will.

"It's all in there," he said. "I copied down Newt's statement word for word. He knew he was dyin', so he'd have no reason to lie. He stated that he was in on the robbery, but was double-crossed by the boss. The man who pulled the trigger was supposed to take a shot at Newt, just to make it look real, but miss. He wasn't supposed to gut-shoot him. I guess the bunch was afraid Newt might get scared, and start talkin', so they decided to kill him and make certain he kept quiet. Their mistake was not makin' certain he was dead on the spot."

"He said that boss double-crossed him, right?" Spurr asked.

"That's right," Mason confirmed.

"That could be anyone, not necessarily Mr.

Kirkpatrick. You'll need more proof than that, Art."

"I'm comin' to it," Mason answered. "Newt told me most of the money stayed right here in town. The men who you ran down were a diversion. The money they took was only their cut. He said the real leader of the outfit was your father, and where to find the rest of the money. I got a warrant from Judge Ralston down in Kerrville to search your family's property. The rest of the money was exactly where Newt said it would be, right under a pile of taters in the root cellar. Your father moved the taters, dug a hole and buried the cash, then piled the taters back over it. I reckon he figured it'd be safe there until things quieted down."

"That doesn't make any sense," Will said. "How much money was in the cellar?"

"A bit more'n ten thousand dollars," Mason answered. "That's the same amount Newt told me would be there."

"That makes even less sense," Will said. "My father said over fifty thousand was taken. Where's the rest of it?"

"He must've hid the rest someplace else, probably because he hadn't been honest with his partners about how much was really gonna be taken, knowin' they'd want a bigger cut. He could easily have slipped that money outta the bank before the robbery."

"But why would he tell everyone there was fifty thousand stolen? That would for certain make folks suspicious, when we caught up with the robbers and only found five thousand on them. My father isn't that stupid. He would have said only five thousand was gone."

"That would only have worked until the next time the state bank auditors showed up from Austin," Mason answered. "My guess is the men who pulled off the actual holdup weren't supposed to get caught. Your trackin' 'em down, and Newt talkin', blew your father's plans sky high."

"I'm still not buyin' it," Will said. "You're positive Newt named my father as behind the whole thing?"

"Sure as I'm sittin' here lookin' at you."

"Max, I'm gonna need to talk to my father again, alone this time," Will said. "After that, I'm gonna do a little more diggin'. Me'n my father might not've seen eye-to-eye, but I'd swear on my ol' horse, Pete, that he had nothin' to do with this holdup. And you know how fond I am of Pete."

"I reckon everyone in town is, Will."

"Good. Jonas, I want you to go to the telegraph office. Send a message to Cap'n Hunter. Tell him we caught the *hombres* who held up the bank, but there's still a few loose ends to be tied up. Meet me back at the house. If you get there before I do, wait for me."

"I'll do just that," Jonas promised.

"I'm obliged," Will said. "Art, you seem to have done a good job figurin' out this case, and I'm grateful. But there's still a couple pieces of the puzzle missin'. I hope you don't take offense at my takin' over for you."

"Not at all," Mason answered. "Your father is a bit of a stuffed shirt, but he loaned my family money when my ma was sick last year, and when she died, he told my pa not to worry about payin' the loan back on time, just get some money to him every month. If I hadn't found that money in the root cellar, I'd never have believed he was behind this, either."

"Thanks, Art. Max, I'm gonna talk to my father now. Oh, before I forget, when's the next stage for Austin?"

"In two days. Why?"

"I'm gonna send a telegram today to my family's attorney in Austin, but I also need to send him a letter explaining the details of my father's arrest, and ask him to arrange bail."

Will went back to the row of cells, shutting the heavy oak door which separated them from the office behind him.

"William," his father said, morosely. "Is there any way you can get me out of this predicament? I didn't want to say anything in front of the others, but things look bad for me, don't they?"

"They do," Will answered. "But don't worry. I know for a fact you weren't involved in this robbery. I'm pretty sure I know who was behind it. However, I'll need your cooperation to prove it. Can I count on that?"

"If you can save me from prison, and clear my good name, I'll do anything you ask, son."

"Good. Can you tell me anything I need to know about that day that you haven't already told Art Mason?"

"Not a thing that I can recall," Silas answered.

"All right. I'll read his report for your statement. In the meantime, I'm going to have to act like I believe you might be guilty, if I have any chance of flushing out the man I'm after. That means you'll have to stay in jail for a little while."

"How long?"

"Two, three days at the most," Will answered. "Can you do that?"

"If it will bring the real mastermind to justice, yes."

"Good. Whatever you may hear in the next day or so, just ignore it. And Father . . ."

"Yes, William?"

"It's more than just a prison sentence you have to worry about. With Newt Haines bein' gunned down durin' the holdup, if I can't force the real culprit's hand, you'll most likely be hung for murder."

· · ·

When Will arrived back home, his mother and Jonas were sitting side by side, in rockers on the front porch.

"William," she cried, rushing down the front walk to meet him. "Jonas has told me what happened. I've been frantic waiting for your return. The whole family has been. Is it true you don't believe your father is guilty?"

"Not for one damn minute," Will answered. "Pardon me, Mother."

"Under the circumstances, your language is understandable," Claudette said. "What are we going to do?"

"I'm gonna prove Father is innocent, and prove who the real culprit is," Will said. "I'm not gonna tell you don't worry, because I know you can't help it. Frankly, I'm worried too. I don't know if I'll be able to find the proof I need or not. But with any luck, I'll have this whole matter cleared up in a couple of days. Can you be strong until then?"

"Of course I can, William. I do hope you can get this straightened out before Susan and Harvey return from New Orleans. It would just about kill Susan to find out her father has been accused of robbery and murder."

"If everything goes right, I'll have Father out of jail and the *hombre* I'm after behind bars well before that," Will answered. "Where are Bertram and Gerard?"

"At the bank, of course."

"Good. I'll need to speak with them once they get home. How about the rest of the family? Where are my aunts and uncles?"

"They're probably still at the hotel, waiting for Buck from the livery stable to pick them up. They agreed to stay with me, once their time at the hotel ran out, since we had no idea when you might be back. They should be here shortly."

"That's great," Will said. "I didn't get as much of a chance to chat with them at the wedding as I'd have liked. Now, if you'll excuse me, Mother, it's been an exhausting few days. I'd like to go up to my room, clean up a bit, and take a nap."

"I think that's an excellent idea, William. You do look a bit peaked."

"If I only look 'a bit peaked' after what I've been through the last several days, then I look damn good, considerin'," Will answered. "Pardon my language again. Jonas?"

"Yeah, Will?"

"I've got a few things to go over with you, then I'm gonna head upstairs."

"That sounds like a fine idea," Jonas said. "I'm plumb tuckered out myself. Soon as we're done talkin', I'm gonna stretch out under that big cottonwood in the back yard, and sleep until tomorrow . . . or at least, 'til suppertime."

14

Two days later, Silas Kirkpatrick still languished in a jail cell, refused bail even to see his brother Samuel, sister Louise, his wife's brother Henri, and their spouses off on their way home. The rest of the Kirkpatrick family was at the Wells Fargo stage depot, except for the honeymooners.

"I've got to go inside and talk to the agent for a minute," Will said. "I'll be right back. The stage won't be rollin' out for a couple more minutes."

He disappeared inside the depot, while the driver and shotgun guard continued to load the passengers' luggage.

"Any more bags?" the driver called out, as he put the last suitcase in place on the roof of the coach.

"I've got one more," Will called from the door of the depot. He came out, carrying a large valise.

"Uncle Martin, you nearly left this behind," he said.

"That's not mine," his uncle answered.

"Sure it is. See, right here on the baggage tag. 'Martin Roberts, Austin, for transfer to Texas and Pacific Railway, through to Shreveport, then connecting to Memphis.' It must be yours."

"There has to be some mistake," Roberts said. "I've never seen that bag before in my life."

"There's one way to find out," Will said. "Shall we open it, and see if the contents belong to you?"

"No. I mean, give me that bag," Roberts ordered. He snatched the valise from Will's grasp. When Will started for his gun, Roberts swung the valise in a wide arc. Its metal reinforced corner caught Will in his left temple.

Will dropped into a pit of darkness, blood streaming from his torn open scalp. He never saw his Uncle Martin start to run, nor heard Jonas's order for him to stop. He never saw his uncle, instead of obeying Jonas's order, spin around as he pulled a gun from inside his jacket, and take a snap shot at Jonas. His bullet tore a hole through Jonas's left arm, then Jonas returned his fire, putting two bullets into Roberts's chest.

Will never saw the valise burst open when his uncle dropped it as he fell to the ground, spilling thousands of dollars in wrapped bills, nor the marshal and deputy have to fire several times over the heads of bystanders who raced to pick up the money. He never heard the shrieking of his shocked family, nor the yells of the Wells Fargo driver as he fought to control his panicked team, and keep them from going into a runaway.

Will just lay where he had fallen, as still as death.

When Will finally regained consciousness, he was in his own bed. Doctor Wilson was with him. He could feel the pressure of a bandage wrapped around his head.

"Will, hello. Good to see you coming around. For a while, it was touch-and-go," the doctor said. "I was really afraid you were going to leave us. I know this is a rather silly question, but how do you feel?"

"Like a horse sat on my head," Will answered. "What the hell happened, Doc? The last thing I remember is my uncle swingin' his case at me, then my head explodin'."

"Let me just do a couple of quick tests first, then, if you seem all right, I'll allow your partner and family in for a short visit. They can explain everything to you, but first, I need to make certain you haven't been concussed."

"I damn sure have been *concussed*," Will said. "My uncle *concussed* the hell out of me when he smashed that case into the side of my head. What the hell happened to him?"

"All right, I need to make certain you haven't suffered a concussion," Wilson said. "As far as what happened after you were knocked out, that can all wait until after I've completed my tests. They'll only take a moment or two." He held up two fingers.

"How many fingers am I holding up?"

"Two," Will answered.

"Good. Do you have any double vision, any blurred vision, or blind spots?"

"No, none."

"Wonderful. Try to follow my finger with your eyes, but don't move your head."

Wilson moved his finger up and down, then left to right and back. Will easily tracked the movements with his gaze.

"Excellent," Wilson said. "What about vertigo—that's dizziness, light-headedness, or nausea?"

"None at all, Doc. How long have I been out, anyway?"

"Just about forty-eight hours," Wilson answered. He listened to Will's heart and lungs with his stethoscope, took his pulse, and checked his temperature.

"All in all, you're healing quite nicely, Will," he said. "Apparently, you just suffered a severe blow to your head. Amazingly, considering where the blow struck, you didn't receive a fatal skull fracture. A week or so's rest and you should be almost as good as new."

"That's good news, Doc. Now, it's high time you told me what happened."

"I'll let your partner explain that to you," Wilson said. "He's waiting downstairs. If you don't think it will tax you too much, I'll allow your family to visit at the same time. I know they still have many questions about this entire affair."

"That'll be just fine, Doc," Will agreed.

"All right. I'll go get them. However, if you

feel faint, or your headache gets worse, have someone summon me immediately."

"You can stay too, Doc. I've got nothin' to say you can't hear."

"I appreciate that, Will. I'll be right back."

Will dozed off while waiting, but was immediately awake when he heard the door open. First in the room was his father, followed by his mother, brothers, and Aunt Louise. Behind them were Jonas, Marshal Spurr, and finally, Peggy and Delia. Will's father came to his side.

"Son, I don't know what to say. . . ." he began. "Can we talk alone for a few minutes?"

"Of course," Will said. "As soon as I find out what happened. I've got some explaining to do to all of you, too. And Jonas, what happened to you?"

Jonas's left arm was in a sling.

"Your uncle tried to make a run for it. When I ordered him to stop, he put a bullet through my arm, that's what happened," he said. "I had to plug him. He's dead. I'm sorry, Will."

"There's no need to be," Will answered. "He got what was comin' to him. He would've hung, anyway. I am sorry for you, though, Aunt Louise."

"There's no need for that, either," Louise answered. "I've already told your partner that."

"Will, I don't want this visit to take too long," Wilson said. "Why don't you just tell your family what you need to for now, then you can fill in the details once you've had more rest?"

"I've already given them part of the story, Will," Jonas said.

"Sure, Doc," Will agreed. "And thanks, pard. Father, as I'm sure Jonas has told you, Uncle Martin arranged the robbery of your bank, then tried to pin the blame on you."

"I know that," Silas said. "But how did you figure out it was my brother-in-law? And no, I don't feel one bit of sorrow at his loss. The man was always a scoundrel. I'm not speaking out of turn in front of my sister, either. Louise has known for a long time what a rotten individual Martin was."

"Two things. The first, which started me on the right track, was when we were ambushed by the gang that pulled the robbery. The man Jonas killed was Michael, Uncle Martin and Aunt Louise's son."

"They already know that, too," Jonas said. "I told them that after everything was over."

"I felt the same about my son as I did my husband," Louise said. "Continue, William."

"Okay. Before he died, Newt Haines told Art Mason that Mr. Kirkpatrick had arranged the robbery of his own bank. Art naturally assumed it was you, Father. Newt was delirious when he gave Art his statement. He must've forgotten Uncle Martin was your brother-in-law, not your brother, so he wasn't truly a Kirkpatrick.

"However, when you said over fifty thousand dollars had been stolen, but Art said only ten thousand was found in the root cellar, and we found only five thousand in the robbers' saddlebags, that confirmed what I'd already suspected when I realized Michael was one of the gang.

"I made some quick inquiries and found out Haines and Uncle Martin had been in touch several times, shortly after Susan's wedding date was announced. They'd planned this scheme very well. If Haines hadn't lived to talk, or if me'n Jonas hadn't caught up with the gang, they might very well have gotten away with it—well, except Uncle Martin decided Haines was a liability, and had him gunned down during the holdup, so Haines never would have had a chance to spend any of the stolen money.

"Once I knew who was behind the plot, I realized Uncle Martin must have had most of the stolen money hidden in plain sight, right here in town. He's the one who cached some of it in the root cellar, then hid the rest in his hotel room. That was another mistake he made—tellin' Haines where he was gonna hide the money. Of course, he figured Haines would never live to talk. If he'd been plugged in the chest, instead of his belly, he most likely wouldn't have, and I'd never have been able to connect Uncle Martin to the robbery, even after me'n Jonas tracked down Michael and the others. And of course he didn't dare identify Michael's body, since that would've connected him to the gang. I couldn't say I knew him, either, since that would have tipped my hand."

"Will, that's enough for now," Wilson said. "One more question, then you need to get some more rest. I know, that sounds like the last thing you need after being unconscious for nearly two days, but you can't afford to overtax your system."

"All right, Doc. Mother, where's the rest of the family? Of course, I know where Susan and Harve are, but—"

"Everyone else is on their way home," his mother answered. "Louise has decided to remain here with us for the foreseeable future. I'm hoping she decides to remain here permanently."

"I probably will," Louise said. "William, this may sound harsh, but there has been nothing but trouble in my home for years. Your uncle was a despicable man. He threw most of his money away on gambling, alcohol, and loose women. I'm certain that's why he wanted the money from your father's bank. I tried to leave him several times, but he threatened my life, so I didn't dare. And Michael was just like him. I lost my husband and son years ago. I feel free for the first time in ages."

"All right, everyone out," Wilson said. "Doctor's orders. Will, you should know that I wanted to keep you at my office for at least a week, but your mother refused. She said there were three women at this house who were more than capable of caring for you."

He looked at Peggy and Delia, and smiled.

"More than capable of bossing me around, and watching me like a mother hen over her chicks," Will said.

"You're right," Wilson conceded. "Now, I mean it. Everyone out."

"Everyone except my father and Jonas, Doc," Will said. "I need to speak with them for a couple of minutes. Then I promise I'll get more rest. I am still feelin' a bit tired."

"All right, but only five minutes," Wilson warned.

"That's all we'll need, Doc."

Will's mother kissed him gently on the cheek, then she and the others, except for Jonas and Silas, left the room. Will's father stood at his bedside, looking uncomfortable and shifting from one foot to the other.

"Will, this isn't easy for me to say," he began. "I understand now why you joined the Texas Rangers. You saved this entire family, son, not just me. We'll all be forever grateful, and we'll be proud to know that you'll be helping others, as you helped us. Your mother and brothers will tell you that once you've rested a bit longer."

"Thanks, Father," Will answered. "I never

thought I'd see the day when you said those words."

"I don't mean I approve of your choice, William, just that I understand. That, and if the day ever does come when you decide to leave the Rangers and settle down, there will always be a home, and a job at the bank, for you here."

"I never expected you to approve, Father, just to understand. That's all I've ever asked."

"You have that understanding now, son. I'd better leave before Doctor Wilson throws me out. Besides, I have to get back to the bank. I'm interviewing replacements for Newt Haines. You take it easy, and I'll see you tonight."

Silas left, closing the door behind him.

"You wanted to talk to me, Will?" Jonas asked.

"I sure did. I just wanted to tell you what a fine job you did on this, your first case for the Rangers. You're gonna be a man to ride the river with. Which is a good thing, since I'll be stuck with you for at least a year."

"I've still got a lot to learn," Jonas said. "And I am sorry I had to kill your uncle. I'm still a bit shaken up about that."

"You'll never get used to havin' to kill a man," Will said. "The day you do is the day you should resign."

"I don't think I ever will," Jonas said. "But I did learn one thing already."

"What's that?"

"Gettin' shot *does* hurt worse'n Delia's medicine."

Will threw a pillow at him.

"Get outta here, before I find my gun and plug you myself," he said, chuckling. "I am gonna take the doc's advice and get some more shut-eye."

"So'm I," Jonas said. "I'm headin' downstairs to my favorite cool spot for a nap, in the shade of that big cottonwood out back. Y'know, it's kinda funny how things turned out."

"What do you mean?"

"You had to kill my cousin, and I ended up killin' yours. Kinda strange, it seems to me."

"Just one of those odd coincidences," Will said. "Call it a twist of fate, or whatever. Things just happen."

"Mebbe I'll contemplate that while I'm nappin' under that tree," Jonas said.

"Enjoy it while you can," Will said. "Soon as I'm mended up, we'll be on our way back to Austin."

"Why am I not surprised?" Jonas said. "Appears we're both fiddle-footed. You get that rest, Will. I'll see you later."

"Later, Jonas."

Once Jonas left, Will laid back on his pillow, with a sigh. It was a bittersweet feeling, knowing he had reconciled with his family at the cost of

251

his uncle and cousin. Still, all in all, things had worked out just fine. He fell asleep with that thought in his head, as a satisfied smile played across his face.

About the Author

Jim Griffin became enamored of the Texas Rangers from watching the TV series, *Tales of the Texas Rangers*, as a youngster. He grew to be an avid student and collector of Rangers' artifacts, memorabilia and other items. His collection is now housed in the Texas Ranger Hall of Fame and Museum in Waco.

His quest for authenticity in his writing has taken him to the famous Old West towns of Pecos, Deadwood, Cheyenne, Tombstone and numerous others. While Jim's books are fiction, he strives to keep them as accurate as possible within the realm of fiction.

A graduate of Southern Connecticut State University, Jim now lives in Keene, New Hampshire when he isn't travelling around the west.

A devoted and enthusiastic horseman, Jim bought his first horse when he was a junior in college. He has owned several American Paint horses. He is a member of the Connecticut Horse Council Volunteer Horse Patrol, an organization which assists the state park Rangers with patrolling parks and forests.

Jim's books are traditional Westerns in the best sense of the term, portraying strong heroes with good character and moral values. Highly reminiscent of the pulp Westerns of yesteryear, the heroes and villains are clearly separated.

Jim was initially inspired to write at the urging of friend and author James Reasoner. After the successful publication of his first book, *Trouble Rides the Texas Pacific*, published in 2005, Jim was encouraged to continue his writing.

Website: www.jamesjgriffin.net

| Books are produced in the United States using U.S.-based materials | Books are printed using a revolutionary new process called THINKtech™ that lowers energy usage by 70% and increases overall quality | Books are durable and flexible because of Smyth-sewing | Paper is sourced using environmentally responsible foresting methods and the paper is acid-free |

Center Point Large Print
600 Brooks Road / PO Box 1
Thorndike, ME 04986-0001 USA

(207) 568-3717

US & Canada:
1 800 929-9108
www.centerpointlargeprint.com